The Royal Diaries

VICTORIA

MAY BLOSSOM
OF BRITANNIA

BY ANNA KIRWAN

Scholastic Inc. New York

ENGLAND, 1829

1 APRIL 1829
KENSINGTON PALACE, LONDON, ENGLAND

This book was not given to me, nor did I buy it with my
own pocket money. You might say that I found it, but that
would not be completely truthful. It is of a convenient
small size, with many empty pages left, having only some
lists of cows written in it here and there. The cover is
brown, mottled paper, and someone has pasted on a white
label. On the label, in very curly letters, it says *Herd
Record.*

For, yes, I <u>stole</u> the book — from an out of the way,
cornermost cupboard in the hall outside the harness
room in the stable. I saw the cupboard swinging open once
a few weeks ago, when I ducked aside to adjust my under-
garments. They were binding me <u>mercilessly</u> before my
excellent governess, the Baroness Lehzen, and I were to
ride out in the carriage. I was itching, so Lehzen bid me go

around the corner privately to compose myself and make myself presentable. (Meanwhile, she watched out for anyone who might accidentally interrupt.)

So I did, and there was a little built-in cupboard with the hook-and-eye latch undone. Inside were ledgers, twenty or so, I should say. One was lists of pigs, by name! One was carrier pigeons; one was geese and guinea fowl and such; several were sheep. None was horses — I should have preferred horses. From whose farm these records were, I know not, save, the years marked on them were between 1813 and 1815, four to six years before I was even born.

When Lehzen and I went out today, I recalled seeing the ledgers last time I was in the harness room. I made the same excuse, to hitch up my petticoat and stockings. (I was wearing the blue ones, and in fact, they <u>were</u> rather stretched out. I fancy the embroidery on them, though.) I slipped quickly into the back hall. And, although it <u>was</u> stealing, I took the ledger. I was dreadfully put to it, to conceal it behind me all the time when I came out. It was tied around my waist with only the sash of my pinafore, and ready to slide loose at any moment!

I don't mean to be unkind, but it almost seemed good fortune for me that Lehzen has had the bad luck to have a sniffling cold this week. She was preoccupied with her nose in her handkerchief on the way back home, and so I managed to fetch in my stolen treasure. I repent <u>sincerely</u> at the bitter knowledge that I have broken a Commandment — still, I trust I have done no other person harm by so doing.

LATER

I had to hide my little journal, as Lehzen came into the room, looking for her pincushion. I stuck my book and my pen under the tapestry footstool.

The reason I hid this ledger is that I do not wish <u>anyone</u> to know that it exists. Really, I must have a place to pour out my curious thoughts privately and sort through them. I never get to be truly alone. Mamma says it would be quite unsafe for a maiden princess to be unguarded by her ladies. So, someone is always nearby — across the room, just out in the hall, in the anteroom. It is not enough that I must sleep in Mamma's bedchamber: I am the only person I know who is not permitted to walk down a flight of steps without holding someone's hand.

Yet sometimes when I am sitting at the window reading or, as now, writing quietly, it is almost as if I am as alone and peaceful as a deer in the forest.

I could be perfectly happy thus, for hours at a time, perhaps, if it were not for the way Certain Persons have of spying on me! I suffer greatly from Their lack of trust. (And now, I fear, my feelings have driven me actually to act against my own conscience — I mean, taking this old ledger in order to defy Their wishes. Though this is a journal, not a letter. They didn't forbid me to write a journal. In fact, They didn't forbid me to write letters, only my own opinions in my letters.)

Of course, if anyone were to give me a pretty little leather-bound journal like the one Mamma's own brother Uncle Leopold keeps, it would only end up being used as a copybook They could read whenever They chose, and then make impertinent remarks. Although I am a princess, His Majesty King George IV's niece Victoria, I am treated this way — with Remarks — too often.

I considered that I might go into the little shop where my art tutor, Mr. Westall, stopped the carriage to buy us lemon squashes to drink that hot day we went out landscape sketching. I might in that way manage to purchase one of the little memorandum books — so charming, with a little pencil attached. But They would know I'd done it, as soon as Captain Conroy made me account for what I'd spent. (Why <u>he</u> must be Mamma's financial advisor and confidential secretary, I do not know!) I'd either be scolded for spending the money, or <u>spied on</u> as to anything I wrote, or <u>both</u>.

How do I know this is so? Because Mamma herself took the letter I was writing yesterday to my darling sister, Feodora. She took it away from that bully, Captain Conroy, at least. In the process of doing so, she behaved every inch the Duchess of Kent and Princess of Saxe-Coburg and Saalfeld.

But then she ripped it up and tossed it onto the fire! Which was, of course, burning low for economy's sake. So I had to watch the pages slowly blacken and shrivel. And I had not made a fair copy of it yet, so it was the only one! I had made it quite an interesting letter, too, for Feo, and I regret that I shan't be able to recall all the remarks as I worded them there. I was in a witty mood when I wrote them, not glum as I am now. I am <u>so</u> vexed!

"These things you write about us and our System here

at Kensington are unbecoming and unkind," is all Mamma said at first.

Victoire Conroy, that traitorous, cowardly snip, the tale-carrier, was so horridly goody-good just then, saying, "I thought it for your safety to tell, Your Highness. Papa says you could be Prey to Others' Interests." Fine words, from someone who reads what one is writing over one's shoulder!

Toire would do or say anything to get her father to think more about her than about me. And I heartily wish he would. He is not my father, he is not even in my family. He is only my dear, dead Papa's equerry, his personal officer — a servant, if one thinks about it. But he is a military man, and Mamma admires the way he orders things. And I am to be persuaded that Their concern for me makes it all right for him to raise his voice and make himself frightful, hammering his fist on the rickety old side table with the twisted barley-sugar-stick legs. He pretends he is angry at my supposed enemies, my "rivals" for His Majesty's favor — mostly my own Uncles! — but I feel as though he is angry at me and at Mamma.

"Your wicked Uncle Ernest would be grateful to be

able to show this to the King!" he accused me. Oh, he was quite beyond his usual, inattentive <u>Oh, hmm, oh, hmm, out of the question!</u> level of temper. Quite! He thundered! "He and the Tories would use it against those of us who have <u>only your interests</u> at heart!" The Tories are the political party for old-fashioned Royal rights, and nothing modern.

And Mamma said, "What you put in writing, Vickelchen, can turn up in the newspapers. You do not understand the need to be . . . to be . . . *Ach, Gott in Himmel — Stille. Ruhe. . . .*"

To which, the baleful O'Hum thundered, "English! English! Speak to her in English! If you want Parliament to ever raise your income, they <u>must not</u> think of her as German!"

Mamma still stood straight as a duchess, but her sweet voice was very meek.

"Victoria, you must understand how to keep <u>quiet</u>, that was the word I wanted, how to be . . . <u>restrained</u>."

Child though I am, I do understand — to a degree. The Royal Family is paid for their services to the nation according to the voting of the House of Lords and the House of Commons. They pay for Mamma and me because of my Duke Papa, but I have so many uncles and aunts and cousins, they do not pay us much. Some of my relatives own estates and treasures, and some have to borrow from their friends.

I hear the grown-up people discuss these subjects, but I suppose I am too young to know what is important. I should be seen but not heard.

But — if I can't tell even Feo my true thoughts, how can she advise me as only a sister can, and console me in my troubles as only a sister can? Hohenlohe is so far away! Why had she to marry? It is <u>very</u> VERY bad when your dear sister has gone to live in a foreign land.

I would give all the rubies in India to be able to talk to Feo right now.

I hear Grampion the footman coming.

LATER

Book under plaid cushion in Fanny's dog basket, just in time. Grampion moved the footstool over by the fireplace, to put my damp boots on. When he went out, I slipped my hand underneath the dog cushion to get my book, and also found the bit of ham bone Cook gave Fanny for barking at the rat in the umbrella stand.

I have been going off, distracted, and did not finish confessing why I got this book. I suppose one reason to write regularly . . . is so as to be certain to tell all. Some days, a great deal occurs. Other days, scarcely anything but weather, hems being let out (or getting tripped on and ripped out), and what sort of pudding was served at tea. I shall attempt to be thorough in thinking about all that happens and what I am learning. I shall have to become a v. fast writer. (For example, that is a fast way to write "very"!)

I am going to hide this diary, where no one will come across it, and I can get it without drawing attention, and write in it. The way today has proceeded, I expect I will have the most chances to write when the bedchamber is quiet and Mamma is abed, after Lehzen has lighted the night-lights and dozed off. I cannot keep it under the mattress, for Lutie or the other maids would find it when they came in to change the linen on Mamma's and my beds. For now, I will slip it behind the big, ugly mauve settee in the upstairs drawing room. No one moves the thing, even to dust, so my book is probably safe there.

When Feo comes back to England, or when I go to

Hohenlohe or Coburg or Vienna as I long to, perhaps to visit Feo and her dear husband, Prince Ernest, there . . . to Feo, I will show this journal. Only to you, darling sister!

See, here is a list of cows' names someone wrote in the ledger:

> *Baby*
> *Dolly*
> *Polly*
> *Pet*
> *Winner*
> *Tully*
> *Nellie*
> *Nancy*
> *Vinia*
> *Rose*
> *Agnes*
> *Vashti*

2 April

It is the most unfortunate thing for a girl not to remember her own father. Dear sister, Feodora, you must know this is so. Even you, who knew your own father for a while when you were small, and then had my own Duke Papa to be, as you said, the best of stepfathers to you and Charles — you must understand what I feel, to have <u>no</u> such store of recollections.

I try to push my memory back as far as I can make it go. Sometimes, I even pray a saint or guardian spirit will bless my memory. I would like to believe it is my own remembering that provides my idea of the tall man whose face filled the sky above my little bed. He speaks toward me, in this dream-memory I have of him, and he says, *Victoire, Liebchen. Victory.* I am not sure I remember him saying, <u>Victoria</u>.

Uncle King is the one who made them call me Alexandrina Victoria, I know. My Papa didn't much like his brother George insisting my first name be in honor of Tsar Alexander — even if he is King George IV of England. Maybe Papa first called me Drina in order not to mix me up with Mamma being "Victoire," and Captain Conroy already naming his daughter for her. Do you remember, Feo? When he died, I was only eight months old. Maybe what I remember is only what Mamma and you and our brother, Charles, and Uncle Sussex have told me. I wish my Duke Papa were still here.

LATER

For breakfast this morning, we had eggs and sausages, and apples and onions fried in bacon drippings, and buns as hard as the back of your head. I asked our dear old de Spaeth, "Baroness, why is the bread so hard this morning?"

She has been Mamma's lady-in-waiting for so many years, she is always at pains to be tactful. She said, "Perhaps it is because Sir John told Cook not to waste anything." I am supposed to call Captain Conroy "Sir John" nowadays, but I shan't, not in my own book.

Later, I asked my tutor, the Reverend Mr. Davys, why Captain Conroy would do such a stingy thing as to deny us fresh bread. Mr. Davys said, "Perhaps because it is Lent." So I didn't say anything about sausages and bacon to Mr. Davys.

Toire Conroy, that sneak, hides behind curtains to listen in, and then tattles. Unless she's lying, the bread was hard because her papa said Uncle Ernest might hire a poisoner if he goes mad, as Grandfather George did, so, there was no soft bread, which might conceal vile tinctures. Victoire says Uncle Ernest murdered his servant.

I said to her, "Did you see him do it?" She said, "No, but everyone says so." I said to her, "I don't say so, so, it's not <u>everyone</u>, is it?" She said, "Your Highness is not <u>everyone</u>. And you are not told <u>everything</u>." I said, "I never said I am. But <u>you</u> must not talk about the Duke of Cumberland, my Papa's big brother, that way." She said, "No, no one must say what you don't like, must they, Your Highness?" But that was not my point.

She says "Your Highness" as if she is spreading treacle on toast. Treacle with ants in it.

LATER

Feo, I asked Charles, who is here for Easter holidays, what he thought of people who put rocks in front of one when one wants a nice, soft, warm bun. Charles just laughed and said, "Why, Schnösel, it's to remind Mamma to write notes to everyone who might notice your birthday's next month."

He means that Captain Conroy is hinting to Mamma that she should write to His Majesty, my Uncle King, that our household requires more income from him or from the public treasury, and that would be a good birthday present for me when I turn ten years old.

I myself would prefer a tame young giraffe, like the

one Uncle King has in his menagerie. Or, possibly, another jewel like the one His Majesty gave me two years ago, with diamonds all around his little portrait painted on a bit of china, like a rose on a teacup. Only, I would rather it be a painting of someone else, someone good-looking. His Majesty is too puffy nowadays, I'm afraid. It is because he has been so unwell. Everyone whispers about his health with dread. I wish with all my heart that it were not so. But his face looks so purple sometimes, he looks more like a bunch of heliotrope than a rose. So, I suppose, diamonds or not, I'd rather have a sweet, dear giraffe, with its cunning little knobby horns.

But, as to O'Hum (my name for Captain Conroy) working for my Duke Papa in the army to begin with, and managing Mamma's budget now and not just the horses, and ordering Cook, and all — they all think I am too young to understand what they are discussing. I think Charles and O'Hum both are dull to Mamma's feelings as a lady and a princess born, and as a duchess, and twice a widow, too, always to have to bring up the subject of the cost of everything. Any enjoyment she might have in meeting with my Father's family is always overshadowed by this matter of the budget. It is not elegant.

Besides, O'Hum is always telling Mamma how spiteful my uncles are, and how jealous they were of my Father. I think Mamma is afraid to vex them with complaints of what things cost, but she is afraid to displease O'Hum by not writing the letters as he thinks she ought. He even makes disapproving remarks about dear Uncle Leopold, Mamma's own brother, who is always so kind to us and so generous. O'Hum says Uncle Leopold does everything little by little and does not know how to get his horse over a hedge. This is not true. Uncle Leopold rides well.

3 APRIL

Rain this morning, and fog. At half past nine the Reverend Mr. Davys came to the drawing room for my morning Bible lesson. We have been reading about Jacob's sons, and how abominably they treated their half brother Joseph. I must say, I am glad Feo and Charles never behaved to me that way! Well, Feo never did. When Charles is around, he does always take sides with a Certain Person. He calls the rest of us "hens." We are not amused by that.

I asked Mr. Davys why all the older brothers were so

jealous of Joseph's coat. Would not the older sons inherit so much more of their father's fortune that one nice coat to wear would not be too much for little Joseph?

But he said, "I believe they . . . ahh . . . they wanted to be the ones to receive their father's blessing."

Then he rustled around in his chair the way he does. It often takes him a while to phrase his answers, and his hair looks like jackstraws by that time. Even Uncle Leopold says he is a lesson in patience.

By and by, Mr. Davys said, "But, perhaps, you know, it was not so easy for Jacob to love the ones who were only eager to have what he'd leave them? Perhaps, not so easy as to love the one who . . . ahh . . . loved him for himself. Expecting no preference, you know."

His hair was sticking out like little bird wings around his ears. I fancied he looked something like Mercury in his winged cap. But even so, he looked very meaningful when he said that. I think he wants me to understand why my Uncle King is so fond of me and so perfectly, stylishly polite and utterly selfish toward Uncle Billy and Aunt Adelaide, and Uncle Sussex, and Uncle Cambridge, and Uncle Cumberland, and His Lordship the Duke of Wellington, and Uncle Leopold, and all.

Of course, Mamma enjoys a degree of <u>almost</u> sisterly affection with my Aunt Sophia, as she does live here in Kensington Palace with us and Uncle Sussex. Mamma says my Papa was sorry for his princess sisters who were never permitted to marry. The whole of Grandfather George III's immediate family is not hostile to us, even though Mamma is a trifle more German in her habits. After all, the Royal Family of England also holds the Throne of Hanover, and that means we are all somewhat German.

But some of Papa's relations are no more fond of O'Hum than I am, I can tell. (Uncle Sussex calls him "that Irishman" — I heard him.) But Mamma is inclined to trust Aunt Sophia's sympathies, because before Papa died, he advised Aunt to entrust matters of her household purse to the Captain. It is unfortunate that Aunt Soap (she doesn't mind my calling her that) tells the Captain <u>everything</u> that is going on.

Uncle Leopold says Papa put "that devil" in charge of his affairs because O'Hum always saw to it that the horses were well kept, at least. And, for Papa, His Royal Highness the Duke of Kent, Uncle says, it was decent logic, because my Papa's military planning was one of his studied strengths.

So, all in all, O'Hum treats Princess Sophia just as sparsely as the rest of us, though she is a princess whose own father was King. But we do have nice horses and carriages. I would be very sorry not to have my mare, Rosa, I know.

I just wish O'Hum would allow Mamma to speak to me in German. I don't know so many words in French, and she is never quite sure what she's saying in English. This may seem an exaggeration, but I constantly feel that if I would like her to hug me, I must be prepared to stand before her and explain what "a hug" is. By that time, some visitor will have sent a calling card in, and there won't be time for her to attend to my request.

By the way — there was soft bread again today at teatime. Toire was probably making it all up, about the poison. I expect she has been reading about the wicked emperors of Rome. I believe their families were treacherous.

LATER

Night-light not quite guttered, Lehzen snoring delicately in her chair. I crept to the maids' closet and got a piece of rushlight to put in the candleholder, to keep the last of the wax burning. I am in the mood to write more about my day, lest I forget.

After lessons and before luncheon, Lehzen and I played dolls. I was going to make the two Dutch peg-dolls we bought last week into opera characters — von Weber's Oberon, perhaps, and Beethoven's Leonore. But instead, we made them into Duke Omar and Duke Zepho. They are in the Bible. They were Joseph's cousins.

Omar had a sort of dressing gown of dark red plush, and Zepho, of Roman-striped ribbon, blue, red, green, and white. (I made Zepho.) We made sashes of gilt soutache trim, and cunning little white head-cloths tied on with black buttonhole thread. I drew Duke Zepho's face with brown ink, and one eyebrow goes up so he looks comical, though I didn't plan that. Lehzen drew Omar in black ink. She says her hand slipped, and he looks like an Italian dandy. But I think he looks more like Mr. Punch in the puppet show at Uncle York's when I was eight.

Katherine is still my favourite doll, though. I tuck her in by my pillow every night.

5 APRIL

Finally! A fair day, warm and pleasant! Mr. Westall, my art tutor, and Aunt Soap and I went outside to sketch in watercolours. The footman, Grampion, went back and forth four times and brought out three India rattan chairs and two easels which, however, we did not use after all, it was so breezy. It turned out to be much easier to work with the drawing board on one's lap, so one could hover over the painting and keep the colours from drying too fast and streaky.

I painted a charming clump of ferns, with a VERY real-looking heartsease next to it, purple and gold with a saffron center like a pheasant's eye. Mr. Westall painted the vista overlooking the linden walk, with the yellow jessamine just opening. He painted it so quickly, but he captures so much perspective with the littlest quirk of his brush! I fear I will always be awkward, compared to his genius.

But the heartsease has a <u>look</u> to it.

Aunt Soap fiddled constantly with the lumpy brooch holding her shawl. She only wears it because my Uncle King gave it to her, not because it's well suited for the task. Other than that, she read the whole time. She does not turn pages very often. I think she is a slow reader. I am a fast reader. She says when she takes me to visit Uncle Sussex in his library, since it is practically on the other corner of the palace, she does not like to hurry right back to our apartments. I can read a good deal in his books without having to bring them back here — and without Aunt Soap catching on that I read so much. It's almost the only way I manage to read any novels for myself.

Mama and Lehzen don't approve of my reading novels. It's not part of the Kensington System of Education. They say I am too young for most fictions, except Mrs. Trimmer. Mrs. Trimmer supposedly writes "improving" stories that will make one a wise child. I think they could use much improving, themselves.

Here's a secret, Feo: Uncle Billy says so, too. He gave me *The Last of the Mohicans* last winter on a Sunday carriage ride, and advised me to keep it hidden in my fisher-fur muff. Sometimes he calls himself Good Old Hawkeye (like one of the heroes in the book), and then he laughs.

"Read now," he said. "Presently, it'll all be nothing but dispatches and newspapers."

I said, "Aye, aye, sir." He liked that. But I wish I could have Mamma's permission to read novels. I want to be good, but I must read stories.

I hope Mamma does invite Lady Northumberland to be my English governess, as she says she might, by and by. Lady N. will be on my side sometimes, I expect. She thinks I am an advanced scholar for one my age. Imagine!

I am afraid I am too lazy ever to be a really scholarly sort.

6 APRIL

Splendid ride this morning! Rosa just about flew!

Currant pudding with wine custard sauce at tea — a rare surprise!

7 APRIL

Not just the post, but a messenger from Windsor Palace arrived this morning! He delivered with pomp a great, thick letter with gilded seals, Uncle King's invitation to go to his ball next month! It came after lessons. Toire and I were playing "actress," dressing up in Grandma'am's old amber-coloured gown *de deux jupes*. (That's French, and it means <u>of two skirts</u>. I must say, Grandma'am's is so vast, it would make <u>two whole gowns</u> for me, but Toire was clever with some ribbons and made it pleat so nicely so I wasn't absolutely swimming in it.)

She took the mauve Spitalfields silk with the dove-grey farthingale and rose-coloured frill. Toire always chuses that one, because I once said I thought it used to be blue, but it faded. She pretends it is blue. I am afraid I cannot pretend about colours. I have no such imagination — to me, a thing either is or is not blue, and one cannot always have one's favourite colour, but why pretend?

While I was in the room, Mamma did not open the invitation. I believe she was put out with Grampion that he brought it in to her while I was not at my studies. I suppose she would have liked to surprise me with the news.

Toire said Mamma most likely wanted to read the invitation first, to see who has been invited, before she decides if I am to be allowed to attend. On my word, it is His Majesty's special invitation! I <u>must</u> attend! They shan't keep me away this year! Surely they shan't! Mamma says she will decide by and by.

I said, "Please, Mamma, decide soon enough so I can have a new dress. I am ever so much taller than I was."

Mamma smiled when I said that. Baroness de Spaeth laughed. "Oh, yes," she teased me, "you've grown the better part of an eighth of an inch!" But I <u>am</u> taller! Quite up to Mr. Westall's waistcoat pocket!

8 APRIL

Everyone here is <u>commanded</u> to attend. I think it is very kind and gracious of my Uncle King to entertain such a large assembly when he has been in such pain. I am told he can scarcely stand, some days. Aunt Soap says no one is more courteous and refined than His Majesty. She says he always found it embarrassing when Grandfather went into one of his peculiar fits. Uncle is consequently exceedingly proper in his own manners.

But Mamma is put out about something, I can tell. She does not think all of His Majesty's friends are quite <u>good</u>. She would not say as much to Aunt Soap, but I believe she thinks my Uncle King, himself, lacks proper behaviour. De Spaeth, bless her, said (I didn't hear it, Toire did) that my own innocence will be adequate protection against any coarse or unseemly impressions. I don't know exactly what it means. I am sure my innocence has not protected me from noting a Certain Person's nose hairs want attention, and that is a coarse impression, I think.

I know Lehzen is passionately eager for me to go to the ball. As she is my governess, I believe she wants me to behave to her credit, and I will certainly try to do so.

Lehzen also said to de Spaeth, "Ivory *peau d'ange* silk for a May evening?" I think that is French for "angel skin" silk — it sounds lovely. And de Spaeth said, "With Honiton lace." They were talking about my dress!

But Mamma still hasn't said yes.

LATER

I am being as good as I can be. I am so cooperative, I am quite a changed little vixen, Lehzen said. That is because it was rather breezy on our ride this morning — my hat blew right off, and my hair was all in knots. Mamma's dresser, Mrs. MacLeod, brushed and brushed my hair before luncheon to get out the tangles. Even though she pulled so hard I thought I should end up bald, I never cried out once. (I am quite ashamed of how I behaved only a few years ago, flinging my boots about, kicking our poor old nurse, Brocky, in her knees if I was even a bit tired when she brushed my hair before bedtime. I was ever so beastly, and she was ever so kind to forgive me.)

I know my dancing instructor, Madame Bourdin, will want me to go to the party. She will want me to be allowed to stay up late and to dance with my cousins, and so to demonstrate how well she has taught me.

As to that, I am of two minds. I do love dancing. And I may say here, in this private journal — think it not conceit, dear Feo! — I am a very fair dancer. No ballerina, of course. But I am not terribly awkward. If only my limbs were a trifle longer and more aerial in their <u>look</u>, I should do quite well. I believe I am sufficiently lively.

But my cousin Georgie will be at the ball. I find him an impossible pig of a boy. He is rude to old ladies with ear trumpets and old gentlemen with ill-fitting wigs. AND he is mean to dogs AND <u>both</u> mean and cowardly toward parrots. AND he says BEASTLY things when the adults can't hear him, and his accent is quite as if he is speaking with his mouth full of tough meat he is still chewing. I should not like to have to spend any part of my magical evening at Court <u>dancing</u> with Georgie!

If only I thought Mamma's concern with WHO will be present were about whether I shall have to dance with Horrid Georgie, I should entirely understand her taking her time making up her mind.

Here are more cows:

1815
Lily, heifer of Livia
Penny, heifer of Pet
Sukie, heifer of Dolly by Bartlet's Bull
Diamond, heifer of Rose
Irene, heifer of Rose
Zubadayah, heifer of Vashti by Bartlet's Bull

9 APRIL

Jellied eels at dinner. Most unspeakable! I begged to be excused. Was not allowed to leave the table. Ate nothing but blancmange and mulberries in syrup. Still had to smell the eels of those sitting near me. Lehzen put caraway seeds on hers, so she will not suffer wind. She puts caraways seeds on her cabbage and her black bread pudding and her cucumbers in cream and her potato dumplings — she puts caraway seeds on everything. She has such a horror of windiness and dyspeptic stomach.

Mamma has not yet said yes about the ball. But my dear Baroness de Spaeth is working at persuading her that it may be good for my position in His Majesty's favour. She let slip a pertinent bit of information, one that must bode well for my wishes, and it is this: The guest of honour at the ball is to be Queen Maria da Gloria of Portugal! She is just my age, so of course I ought to be able to meet her!

This is how the conversation went. The Baroness was sitting with Lehzen and me in the yellow drawing room before dinner. Lehzen was reading a volume of Schiller's poems. De Spaeth and I were decorating little round cardboard powder boxes, cutting bits of fabric to fit, gluing the edges down, then trimming them with gold braid and velvet florets from old bonnets.

I did mine with pale peach-blossom Shantung silk (left-over from Aunt Adelaide's new dressing room drapery.

She brought me a little scrap bag full of lovely little snippets of it. She is <u>so</u> thoughtful.)

The Baroness was doing hers in lilac moiré. Somehow, old ladies always seem to choose lilac or lavender for everything. Mourning colours, I say. I suppose by the time one is advanced in age past forty or so, one's whole life is demi-mourning. "One peg in the grave" is what Uncle Billy says, but he is rather older than that and is perfectly spry.

However that may be, the Baroness had just showed me how to pull a puff of cotton quilt batting thin across the top of the box and paste it down to provide a nice padding under the silk. The effect is quite elegant.

I said to her, "I do so <u>love</u> pink! If only Mamma would let me wear a pink frock in company sometimes, not always white!" Truly, I was not thinking particularly of Uncle's party, only making a general comment.

My good de Spaeth, though, spoke with great seriousness.

"Your Highness must realize it would not be suitable for you to dress in the same fashion as Her Majesty Doña Maria. <u>You</u> are an <u>English princess</u>."

"Why, who is Doña Maria?" I said. "How does she

dress? As I don't know her, I had hardly thought of mimicking her!"

And the Baroness de Spaeth said (as she daintily wiped a bit of paste off her fingertips — she is so much neater than I!), "Well, you know <u>who</u> Her Majesty is, of course, the little Queen who is coming to His Majesty's feast! But she is a <u>Queen</u>, though she is a little maiden like yourself. And Portuguese, as well — quite Brazilian, they say — you know, southern taste is quite elaborate. But white frocks suit the little English May Blossom, still."

She is just like my Grandmamma Coburg, calling me "May Blossom" and "May Flower" all the time. I liked it better before Horrid Cousin Georgie told me it was the name of a leaky traitor ship that went to America. I don't think that rude boy knows what he is talking about, but just the fact that I think of him now every time anyone says "May Flower" rather spoils it for me!

But when I was thinking it over later, it occurred to me that I <u>am</u> the most suitable person to keep Doña Maria company. Even if she is a Queen and I am only a daughter of a duke who has already passed away and can never be King. My birthday is so close to hers. It must be nice to be turning ten years old and have the Monarch of England give a birthday party for one! Perhaps some year there will be no important Visitors of State at hand in May, and my Uncle King might chuse to give me a party. I am sure I would be grateful if he did.

10 APRIL

Today, Toire and I played "actress" again. But Toire says we must not call it that, it isn't proper, because Actresses are not Ladies. She says we should call it "Playing Cameos."

At first she was going to be a prioress, a nun. She pinned a white tablecloth around her throat and then put de Spaeth's black crocheted shawl over her head, and she had on a black dress.

Toire's face is much more dramatically shaped than mine. Mine is shaped like a roly-poly pudding. And my mouth is crooked.

Her face is more pointed and foxlike.

I wanted to pretend to be Rowena the Saxon, because I have been secretly reading another novel, *Ivanhoe,* by Sir Walter Scott, a poet who has come to visit Mamma and Uncle Sussex. Rowena is one of the characters in the story.

I dared not confess as much to Toire, she's such a tattler. And she has plenty of nosiness! But she has so little curiosity — I mean, real curiosity. She never asks where my ideas come from. I don't know if there is a prioress in the book, I am not finished reading it yet.

LATER

A close call — Lehzen almost caught me writing. I sat on my book so quickly, I feared I got ink on my skirt, and had to go check in the looking glass. But I suppose I whisked my book out of sight so fast, the breeze dried the ink directly!

To return to my account: When Toire could not persuade me to be a nun with her, she considered being a Lost Sheep Saved. Then she decided she'd change her name to Sister Mary Margaret, and she declared herself to be a Belgian mystic saint. For such a sneak and liar, she certainly has very <u>holy</u> fancies! She did not seem in the mood for me to propose to her that she be Rebecca the Jewess of York, but there are no other girls except those two in *Ivanhoe* yet, so far as I've read. So I said that I would be both Rowena and Rebecca and she could be a Belgian prioress.

Really, I was rather glad that she wouldn't make a good Rebecca. The truth is, Rebecca is more interesting than Rowena. Though I dare say I <u>look</u> more like Rowena. For Rebecca, I wound Lehzen's yellow scarf 'round and 'round my head, with de Spaeth's ruby brooch to hold it like a turban. For Rowena, I made a wreath of primroses (THAT took some time) with a silvery silk gauze scarf over it that fell over my face. Mrs. Arbuthnot was visiting Mamma and offered me the loan of the scarf without my asking — a very kind loan, I think. I was careful with it.

I like to make up speeches and act out whole scenes, but Toire prefers to do a tableau, just a scene with no moving or speaking, because she is better at holding still than she is at remembering her lines. Also, she is better at holding still than I am. Of course, I could MAKE her do as I wish. She is the one who is always talking about my "precedence," my right to be treated with Utmost Respect. She is her father's little parrot. But she forgets her lines and so often says "Um, um, I shall recall it all momentarily," it drives me daft. I vow, when Lehzen says I am willful and always expect to have my way, she has no idea how often I bite my tongue and hold myself in where Toire is concerned!

So, perhaps we will do a tableau at tea tomorrow, if Mamma will let us be actresses in company. Or cameos.

LATER

To my great joy, I believe Uncle Leopold will be dining with us tomorrow.

His last letter to me was so lovely. "*Dearest Little Child, I have travelled far over the world and shall be able to give you some curious information about various matters.*" Mamma does not invite him often to Kensington, although he is her own brother. I wonder why she is sour about him this time. It's O'Hum's fault, I am sure of that much. I hear him blustering and vowing this and that about how much income Uncle has to share. It is not as though dear Uncle planned the death of his wife, my poor Aunt Princess Charlotte, or Parliament's grant for them being greater than what my Papa had.

Toire says my Duke Papa left so many debts because he was too charitable. She also says perhaps she would really like to be a nun instead of getting married, because of what happens when people try to have babies. She meant Aunt Charlotte dying in childbirth so tragically young. De Spaeth overheard. She said, "Nonsense, it's these English doctors thinking they can cure everything with their filthy leeches."

Sometimes, Feo, I really feel sympathy for poor Victoire. But then she does something repugnant.

When I told her I was Rebecca the Jewess of York, she said, "Oh, Your Highness, how <u>shocking</u>, how <u>can</u> you, and so close to Easter, and with His Grace Dr. Howley the Archbishop of Canterbury calling during the day?"

I wish she had not reminded me. His Grace gives me a bad case of nerves. Lehzen laughs at me when I say so, but it is true and of course dreadful, and I can scarcely manage to stay courteous. When I was little, I thought at one time that his name was Dr. Holy and another time that he was a ghost, Dr. Howling. Then I thought for a while that he was the one the Bible referred to when it spoke of the Holy Ghost arriving like tongues of flame (I believe that was the year Uncle Billy had Hindoostani fire-swallowers at his garden party at Bushey, too — quite horrid when one is small!). I feared for several days that the candles in church were to be used to light our mouths on fire. I believe I must have had a bad dream about these words because I didn't understand them. It was silly, but I still rather fear the Archbishop, and I shall wait until he is gone before proposing to show Mamma our tableau.

But, about Rebecca the Jewess, Feo. I realize that Toire has never gone with us and Uncle Leopold to Mr. Montefiore's at Ramsgate, where Mamma takes us for our summer holidays by the sea. I am afraid she is not what Uncle would consider fair-minded, or she would appreciate that Mr. M. is so kind to let us play in his garden, and he is a Jew, and is perfectly amiable. I am sure no one could take exception to him, who knew him. But she was behaving quite in a <u>medieval</u> way, if one thinks about it. And I know she thought she was being especially pious. Imagine!

I wonder what the Reverend Mr. Davys would tell me about playacting the part of Rebecca during Easter season.

12 April

Uncle Leopold was indeed here for Sunday dinner yesterday. I was allowed to come to the table with the grownups, although Lehzen made it clear I was not to dominate any portion of the conversation, but to listen to how it is done among the best society.

Our dear, <u>dear</u> Uncle is the most fascinating individual in the world, I believe. He is very handsome, with those fine, dark eyes of inexpressible kindness. He has to be so brave, carrying the burden of his sorrow for losing his beloved wife, Aunt Charlotte, the way he did. He says she was always lively and merry.

I cannot but notice, though, that Uncle does not overload his conversation with sad sentiments. During the several courses of our meal, for example, he spoke of many things, subjects introduced by himself or others.

Uncle brought me a present, too — a lovely brass nutcracker, made in the shape of a griffin with a lion's mane and an eagle's beak. "These English walnuts are the most hardheaded crop in Europe," he said. That made Lehzen laugh so, she turned quite pink.

22 April

Roast leg of lamb, garnished with mint jelly moulded into the shape of strawberry leaves, and also roast pork with herbs crusted to the cracklings, and soup with parsley dumplings, and watercresses, and a pineapple, and coconut cake, and ices.

That was dinner yesterday.

In the morning, we went to the Abbey in the barouche, our most stylish carriage, and came back by way of Rotten Row. I bowed my head to everyone who bowed to me (everyone, in other words!) and said, "A Happy Eastertide to you." I was wearing my white serge coat, as the day was charmingly warm, and my new bonnet with blue ribbons and white egret tips.

After we arrived back home, Mamma said I may go to the ball! Now, I only pray nothing might happen to cause her to change her mind. (I mean: a Certain Person of wrathful looming-overness.)

Really, I cannot understand how there could have been any question whether I should go, as we are commanded, rather than invited. Toire, in her most KNOWING manner, told me that is EXACTLY why her papa and my mamma had to consider carefully.

I replied (rather irritated) that my mamma knows there can be no serious question! I am a princess, but I am His Majesty's MOST LOYAL subject!

Toire looked entirely too smug at that. She said, "Pity, then, he's not so fond of you as you seem to think. He's chusing <u>your</u> birthday week to give a party for someone else! And one who but recently lived in Brazil, at that. Papa says that is a 'gross insult,' <u>Your Highness</u>."

I felt as though she had slapped me. I could not understand why she wanted to be so cruel.

Afterward, though, I found out. Everyone is NOT invited. Toire is not. She says she doesn't care, for the people at Court wear too much perfume and pomade, and her lungs are delicate. (A lie.)

If she went, maybe she would do some of the dancing with Cousin Georgie, and I wouldn't have to. She could ask <u>him</u> if his father, Uncle Ernest, murdered his manservant.

But it really does not seem fair she can't go.

24 April

Tried <u>four</u> times to write, but almost got caught each time. My heart spends a good deal too much time in my throat these days.

However, I have found that some of my best times for writing are very early in the morning, when the birds are just starting to sing. I can sit by the window, with my down counterpane wrapped around me. I write with a pencil, for I dare not try to manage an ink bottle in such a position.

Another time I have found that often allows for a spot of writing is after breakfast, if Mamma is indisposed, and I am set to working by the globes in Uncle Sussex's library. I make my lists of principal seaports and northernmost outposts and so on, and I do it promptly and rapidly as soon as I am seated. They think it will take me a half to three-quarters of an hour to fulfill the task. But I write as quickly as the Captain does, and with a good deal less time wasted on flourishes.

I was too tired to write all that happened yesterday. I was too sleepy at bedtime. I thought I would go get my book, but before Lehzen dozed off, <u>I</u> did. I'll try to catch up when next I can write.

LATER

We went to the Serpentine pond in Hyde Park in the afternoon, and Uncle Billy let me sail his model of the *Pegasus*, his old Navy ship, in the pond where all the boys from Eton were sailing their boats. Aunt Adelaide was quite beside herself, and I did get my shoes damp. We tipped the boat over once in a gust, and Uncle said sailors' words. Then, as my commanding officer, he ordered me to forget what he said.

One of the boys had a boat that was supposed to be Admiral Nelson's ship, the *Victory*. The Admiral was a great friend of Uncle Billy's, and he died a great hero. I believe Uncle misses him a good deal.

6 MAY

It is so provoking, but there's no help for it. Mamma lets me do nothing wherein I might breathe bad air — but lately she includes <u>fresh</u> air in her ruling! She is so particular this week about my not catching a cold. Since it's how my dear Papa caught his death, of course I take the matter seriously.

I am not a careless infant. Uncle's friend, Dr. Stockmar, says pure air is of utmost importance in maintaining one's health. He is the one who told Mamma to put white upholstery in her apartments and watch it for soot and mildew, to know if the chamber is wholesome to live in. It is useful advice, although Captain Conroy rumbles, "Oh, hmm, one more way to waste money, and nothing to show for it."

I came in panting after a brisk canter, and I suppose I looked flushed. Mamma wanted to feel my forehead and put a shawl around my shoulders while I did my geography recitation, which I couldn't have borne. Egypt makes one warm enough.

De Spaeth whispered to me, as she tried to help with my soaked bootlace, "You cannot go to Court with a cold. Your Mamma will not permit it."

I asked Mamma and O'Hum if Toire could please come to the ball. I said I would send my Uncle King a charming note, and ask it as a favour for my birthday. Mamma looked confused. O'Hum didn't look at me at all. He said, "Oh, hmm, not necessary, not at all necessary."

I was glad I hadn't told Toire I would ask. It would be too hard to explain.

LATER

Mamma and Lehzen and I have had letters from Feo in to-day's post. It is so charming to hear of life in Hohenlohe. I wish we could go and stay with her sometime. It sounds so amusing, the way she speaks of managing her own household and staff.

Compton, everyone's favourite sewing maid, is cutting out my dress today. She's using the same pattern as my (favourite) lawn frock that has eyelet lace trim, only adding another inset panel to make it longer. (I really <u>am</u> taller.)

Greta, the new girl, was helping. She got nervous while fitting the muslin pattern on me, and accidentally ran a pin into my leg. I thought she would just about die. I saw tears in her eyes, she was so distressed! It was only a pin, after all. And I am a soldier's daughter.

I would have said a few words to comfort her, but Lehzen was reading a fairy tale to me the whole time, "The Twelve Dancing Princesses."

29 MAY

I celebrated my tenth birthday five days ago. Yesterday I attended the Royal ball. So much has happened! Alas, I've had no time to write. Now that I am ten years old, I must learn to be stricter with myself. It would be unfortunate to have one's failings known publicly. At Court, one is under EVERYONE'S eye.

The most amazing thing is this, dear Feo: I rather like it. I don't know why dear Mamma thinks it's not nice there. I watched all the lords and ladies bow to one another and say such pleasant things. They dress BEAUTI-FULLY, of course. It is like a conservatory of satin and sheared velvet and gauzy silk *chiffoneries*, all the hues of petals, seashells, pastry icing. I never saw so many ropes and knots and stars of shining jewels! The candlelight glimmered on the golden epaulets as if they were the armour of the most splendid company of knights. The gleaming scarlet and black of the military uniforms looked like a pack of playing cards scattered all around.

And the music was HEAVENLY. Not only was there an orchestra that played for the dancing, but also violins and a cello on the terrace. A female harpist played in the ladies' withdrawing room. The evening being mild and clear, Scotch bagpipers in their plaid kilts were marching here and there out in the gardens, playing "like a topping gale," Uncle Billy said. I could tell he meant that as praise.

It was not true, what Toire said about my Uncle King not noticing my birthday, as I shall tell.

When I went up to make my courtesy to His Majesty, I was quite nervous. I had to kiss His Majesty's hand. Really, one kisses the air <u>over</u> his hand, and that's a good thing, for he's so glistening with lotions and powders to cover the liver spots on his skin, which he hates. (I heard him say so to Lady Conyngham. Perhaps, also, the Royal purpleness, though he didn't mention that.)

Aunt Soap says he was a beautiful lad when he was young. "Prinny was the handsomest Prince ever. His curls were the colour of honey on toast, like that red-gold Russian sable the Princess de Lieven wears." Now, unfortunately, his beauty has quite fled. Perhaps he does wear a corset, as I once heard Lady C. remark — though I can't see that it does much good. (I'm sure she would be shocked to know I overheard. But I do wonder why so many people seem to think a young person's ears do not work unless they are instructed to by some adult.)

When I had kissed the air above His Majesty's hand,

which was scented with eau de cologne, he leaned over the arm of his chair, quite sideways. Feo, he's so bulgy, he <u>can't</u> bend forward very well! But he leaned over and held his cheek toward me and patted it with his big, plump hand, which is the size of a plucked quail, and loaded with rings like cherries. He said, "You pretty little pet, give us a true kiss, now."

So I did, though he was rather pink and white and greasy with makeup. His hair smelled like gardenia, almost <u>overpowering</u>.

Then he said, "Ah, so charming. Now, hold out your little paw. I have something for you." (His Majesty <u>always</u> calls my hand a "paw," so I think it's not <u>too</u> terrible to call his a quail, is it, Feo?)

He rang a little bell then, and a footman stepped up and bowed and handed him a flat, square, green velvet box. Uncle held it out to me and said, "My dear, a very, very happy birthday." Really, it was four days after my birthday, but he was close.

I was not certain if I should open it then and there, but of course I said, "Oh, Your Majesty, thank you. You are so kind to me."

"And you, at least, can see that, can't you," he murmured.

"How difficult can it be?" (And I believe the glance he cast past my shoulder was aimed at poor Mamma, who had been announced when we entered the ballroom, but to whom he had not yet said a word.) "Open it, open it," he bid me.

So I did, and it was the loveliest little necklace of pearls, so delicate, with a cunning clasp of tiny diamonds spelling G.R.A., which you know means George Rex Anglorum — George, King of England.

"Help her on with it," he commanded Lady Montagu, who was standing nearby. When she had it fastened, he said something that touched me deeply. He wiggled a finger at me to come closer, and then he whispered, "Don't tell anyone at home, but that was my daughter Charlotte's. His Majesty, my father, gave it to her when she was just your size. You are better behaved than she was, poor little soul — you won't pop the string, will you?"

"Oh, no, dear Uncle King," I vowed. "I shall treasure it." I was <u>thoroughly</u> astonished: I believe there were tears in his eyes. However, the ballroom was a very glittering place, so I may have been mistaken.

At that moment, Uncle Cumberland was announced,

and His Majesty said, "Run along, then," and I did something I did not expect of myself. I stepped up next to him and kissed his cheek again. I truly meant it, too. Poor old King. I have no Papa anymore, and he has no daughter.

Then I backed away hastily, for I didn't want to have to kiss Uncle Cumberland's ghastly cheek, with his eye all puckered out of place and nasty from the saber scar. And of course, my full-of-himself cousin Georgie was with him, too.

I have so much more I want to write, Feo. I want to remember every detail and share it all with you. But I cannot continue now. Mamma wants me to come say "how do you do" to Lord Brougham and some other visitors. I suppose it is my duty.

LATER

Back again.

Then was announced Her Majesty, Maria da Gloria, Queen of Portugal. Oh, Feo, I can scarce describe to you the splendour of her whole demeanor and person!

Her hair is black as a swallow's wing is, almost blue in its highlights, and she was wearing a delicate crown that looked quite old. Her gown was of crimson velvet, rather stiffer than we wear our gowns here, but perfectly elegant. It had bands of gilt embroidery down the front of the skirt, too, and around the hem. She was wearing <u>many</u> jewels.

Her face is quite serene and very strong, I think, for a girl. It is rounded but not round, and her skin like ivory — old, creamy ivory.

Lehzen looked at Her Majesty, I can only say, <u>shrewdly</u>. I do not mean unkindly. "That child," she murmured. "To think, they are already discussing a marriage contract. . . ." Of course, I was very interested to learn *that*, but Lehzen would say no more.

We had not made our whole progress back to our corner of the ballroom when Uncle King sent his little African page to bid me come to the reception line to greet Her Majesty Queen Maria.

And, as luck would have it, I was just behind Georgie, who does not know how to whisper invisibly, but thinks he does.

"Oh, you're here, Wigglechin?" he said first. I could see from his smile that he meant to be annoying. He knows

I do not permit <u>anyone</u> to call me "Vickelchen" anymore, except Mamma; and she is not so fond of me, now that I'm older — lately, she only uses it to correct me. So, it is a baby name by which I can no longer abide to be addressed under <u>any</u> circumstances — especially in the reception line within so short a distance from such splendid, charming people. Among whom I cannot count Georgie.

The next thing he said was, "I hear she does her hair with sardine oil." He was speaking of Her Majesty.

"Lie," I said to him. "She doesn't, and you didn't hear any such thing. Two lies."

Then I cut him no more attention, and turned to greet Her Majesty's ladies-in-waiting, her ministers who are traveling with her, and, finally, Her Majesty, herself — the heir of Henry the Navigator! My heart thrilled to think of it!

"Your Majesty," I said, dropping my curtsy, and she said, "Your Highness, I am honour and please to salute you." That seemed to be the whole extent of her English, but her French is better, so we conversed <u>briefly</u> in French. She said she admired the band. "That was Mendelssohn, was it not?" It was, from *A Midsummer Night's Dream*. I said, "Yes, we are fond of his music here, indeed, we are." Then she nodded to me, and I passed on to her chancellor, who stood next in line. Her Majesty and I also spoke together several more times during the evening. She is a very pleasant girl, Feo, and seems warmhearted and affectionate and honest.

She was wearing a very, very pretty neck chain of coloured gems. But she was also wearing a very exquisite necklace of star sapphires, a gorgeous ultramarine blue, and it had a clasp that said G.R.A., too, but the clasp was not as old-fashioned as mine.

After everyone had gone through the line, I went to the withdrawing room with Lehzen, before the dancing began, and I overheard Lady Peel say the Queen's necklace was His Majesty's present to her. Imagine that, Feo!

Then I heard something I did not like to hear. Another lady said that she was shocked to see how weak and old His Majesty has become this past year. She said she would not be surprised if he is "done for before Christmas."

The saddest part, Feo, was, not one of the ladies to whom she said it seemed to disagree.

So lovely. I wish I could just run outside barefoot and roll on the grass the way my little horse, Rosa, does. What good is it, being a princess, if you don't get to run barefoot on the first of June?

I don't want to forget anything that happened at the ball, so I continue.

Mamma had been through the reception line, too, behind me, and had come back to our corner of the ballroom. When she saw my necklace, she pursed her lips, and I knew she thought sapphires were the better present. But I think the sapphires are just something new from some jeweler's shop. I wish my Uncle King hadn't forbidden me to tell that my necklace was Aunt Princess Charlotte's.

But Mamma did say they are uncommonly well-matched pearls.

Then the dancing began, and at first I only watched. But, by and by, Lord Elphinstone led me up for the quadrille, and it was SHEER BLISS. I knew all the figures and steps, and if we did not exactly <u>romp</u> (after all, we were at Court!), we certainly did <u>sail</u> from one to another. The orchestra played long enough for the whole company to make it through to the promenade before they closed the tune.

For that first dance, my Uncle King led Her Majesty through the first dos-à-dos, and then had Admiral Sir George Cockburn finish the dance with her. His Majesty's gout is very painful when he stands. Admiral Cockburn towered above Her Majesty, though, and they were an odd pair, like a stork dancing with a swan.

Oh, of all places. More cows on the next page. One may remove the book from the barn, but one cannot avoid the barn in the book.

> *Guernsey: Rose, Diamond, Winner, Irene*
> *Holstein Friesian: Tully, Nellie, Pet, Penny, Sloe*
> *Ayrshire: Agnes, Nancy*
> *Jersey: Molly, Polly, Dolly*
> *Jersey x Aberdeen: Sukie*
> *Brown Swiss: Vinia*
> *Dutch Belted: Melchett, Livia, Lily*
> *Red Polled: Vashti, Hazel*
> *Red Polled x Aberdeen: Zubadayah*
> *Aberdeen Angus: Bartlet's Bull*
> *Guernsey: Ch. Castle Hill Aurylius*

Later

Now, sadly, Feo, I must tell you something so shocking, I know it will afflict you to hear of it, though you are so far away. You will blush for me, for this involves VERY BAD BEHAVIOUR of one of my own relations. I am sorry to be so connected. Of course, I mean Georgie Cumbersome. (I suppose I am being vulgar to call him that. But judge for yourself.)

My Uncle King chose Georgie to stand up next with Her Majesty. Georgie led her up to the next dance. But he danced like a bear at the circus, too slowly for the measure, and then he realized they dawdled so the figure was too uneven, and then he galloped to catch up. He cared nothing for Her Majesty Doña Maria's high-heeled satin slippers (she is hardly taller than I am), and he yanked her along as if she were a stubborn donkey, and ended up knocking her right over!

It was perfectly dreadful, for she got a great, purple black-and-blue bruise on her cheekbone, and her skirt had bootblacking on it when she arose, so she retired early.

And that beastly Georgie said it was <u>her</u> fault, that she

<u>should</u> have been watching where <u>she</u> trod, and that she had no sense of the music! Then he went off to the refreshment alcove and proceeded to spill a cup of syllabub on his lace cuff, so it looked like a berry netting after a bad rain.

And yet he thinks so well of himself.

Now I am glad Baroness de Spaeth advised against my wearing raised heels, though they would have made me taller for the dancing.

During the rest of the evening, I danced with Prince William of Saxe-Weimar (v. good-looking, but shy), Prince Esterhazy (passable dancer), Lord Fitzalan (he will be the next Duke of Norfolk — he was amusing), and the sons of Lord De la Warr (v. pale golden hair, bluebell blue eyes), and Lord Jersey (dark curls, blue eyes, v. witty, with a handsome nose). It was a good deal of fun to be among so many persons near my own age.

Then, fie, I had to dance with the Disastrous Swine of Cumberland. I saw immediately that he had chosen to refresh himself with grenadine ice, for now his <u>other</u> cuff was likewise <u>defiled</u>, and I feared for my Honiton lace. I dreaded dancing with Georgie.

"Did you see her — Queenie, there — go down on her precious phiz?" he began. (He meant her face.) "She's a cow. They'll have to put leeches on her face to clear that bruise off," he said, and he laughed in a nasty way.

"They'll put a caraway poultice on it," I said. Mamma doesn't let them leech my bruises, but I didn't say that to Georgie. His father, my Uncle Cumberland, thinks Mamma's medical ideas are radical.

LATER

I had to cease my writing for a while, as Mamma came looking for the inkwell. That was a narrow escape. Then it was time for breakfast. Now I am writing while Lehzen writes letters. Mr. Davys has an appointment with his sister's physician, and will arrive by and by.

What happened next at Uncle King's ball:

Oh, let me remember. Oh, yes:

"Leeches," George said again when we were partnered once more. He was getting so much out of breath from exertion, spittle was in the corner of his mouth. Georgie is disgusting. "They'll bleed her like they did that strumpet, Princess Charlotte. And your old dad. They say they took a gallon of blood from him, and he died anyway."

I hate Georgie Cumberland. He is a wicked boy.

Of course, I would not say so. It is important that I remind myself that I know so much better how people ought to be treated and spoken to.

I am older than he is, of course. He is still only nine.

By and by, I danced with Uncle Billy, but Georgie had set me so at sixes and sevens, I was quite pouting, I'm sure. I was growing tired, too, as you may imagine. So Uncle danced a bit of a hornpipe to make me laugh. In the darkest spot, my Uncle Billy is like a ray of sunlight. Do you remember him that way, Feo? Probably not. But so he is. He knows how to talk with children.

And I do believe Lord Elphinstone was approaching me again to ask for another dance, only Uncle Leopold stepped up, clicked his heels, and offered me his arm.

Looking closely at my necklace, Uncle Leopold said, "Before you are a year older, you must ask your Uncle King for two more pearls each year you are growing, so it won't choke you to wear that sign of his fondness. You must cause him to remember how quickly girls grow up. That is what you must do, my dear."

Lehzen came into the room. Then she went out into the hallway to talk to the laundry maid about starch in the bedding. I took up my big atlas and have it open in front of me, and am writing that way, with my journal inside. It is so awful to be always dreading discovery.

But to continue:

A great row at breakfast. I was still tired from the ball, and so was Mamma. She cannot say anything pleasing about my Uncle King's gift to me. But I'm sure I would get on better with her if it were not for That Man.

The third time Mamma called them "only pearls," I was growing rather warm on the subject. O'Hum was making it sound as if I had bungled things, to have no more to show for all our trouble — as if a Royal ball were trouble!

"Baroness de Spaeth says pearls are <u>most</u> suitable for a child my age," I said. Mamma said the sapphires would have matched my eyes. Then I was very naughty. "Oh, fie," I said. "Cannot you say, just as well, the pearls match my teeth?"

"Pert tongue!" That Man said. "The governess shall be instructed to snip it with her scissors!"

Oh, horrid, horrid, horrid! "You are worse than my Uncle Cumberland!" I cried out.

"Your Royal Highness," he thundered at Mamma, looming over her as he does, "I am sure it would be best for you to tell the princess to be silent, as befits her age!"

So I said what Uncle Billy said in the House of Lords about Uncle Cumberland.

"This is England, not Hanover. Here we say what we like."

I am afraid I stomped my foot when I said it.

Mamma began to cry, and Lehzen told me I must beg Mamma's pardon. So I said I was sorry, but Mamma shook her head and waved her hand and didn't quite take her face out of her handkerchief as she said, "Yes, yes, of course you are — now."

Lehzen took me away, and the last thing I heard as I left the breakfast room was O'Hum banging his fist on the table, shouting at Mamma, "Lot of nonsense! Wipe your face, Madame, you'll spoil your looks! Mr. Coutts will be here in a quarter of an hour!"

I hate Captain Conroy.

6 JUNE

Bad news has led to good, dear Feo. I am sitting up late writing. Lehzen will not interrupt me. This is what has happened.

I was very sorry to have behaved so badly to Mamma. Truly, I believe she has enough to bear. That morning I acted so bold and common and angry toward her, she retired to the rose sitting room and lay down on the fainting couch and allowed no one to come to her except de Spaeth. I was so ashamed of myself, I felt very low.

O'Hum went off downstairs to meet with Mr. Coutts, the banker. I later heard Aunt Soap tell Uncle Sussex that O'Hum was even more irritated when Mr. Coutts left. He wanted to buy six new, matched Irish bays for the carriages before we go down to Claremont to visit Uncle Leopold next month. But Mr. Coutts would not agree to it.

I admit that gave me some satisfaction. My Duke Papa was a soldier, but I am sure he would never have forgotten himself so as to order Mamma about! Why is it all right for That Man to treat a Duchess worse than we ever would treat Cook or Compton or even Grampion? I do not understand adults very well.

I was miserable and stupid during my lessons with the Reverend Mr. Davys. Toire came in, clicking and clacking her knitting needles and counting stitches under her breath, so one could hear her. It is a special talent she has, being quiet noisily. She said to Lehzen, so clearly that I'm sure Mr. Davys heard, that Mamma sent her out of the sitting room because my flying into such a passion had given her a headache.

The Reverend Mr. Davys said "Harrumph" a few times, and then excused himself to go briefly to the lounge to smoke a pipe.

Then Lehzen told Toire she should go upstairs to the unused drawing room until it was time for music lessons. Of course, I could not let that happen, because my journal was up there, and I was in agony lest Toire should discover it! No doubt, she could trade it for a whole thimbleful of attention from her father. And then I'd get the whole, cold, North Sea's worth. Not a pleasant thought.

So I pretended to have a coughing fit, and Lehzen sent Toire to fetch me a drink of water. I whispered desperately to Lehzen, to please not send her to that room. Lehzen gave me a sharp look, but she is such a kind, wise, dear friend, she saw I had some reason she could not discover just then, but even so, she honoured my request.

In that moment, Feo, I realized, just as you said — Lehzen is my true friend. Even though I had been so wicked at breakfast, she trusted that my heart was changed since then, and she took care of my wish. When Toire came in with my water, Lehzen told her it was too musty upstairs for her lungs, and she would be better off sitting in the window seat of the yellow room. Poor Toire is always glad when she gets attention for her frailties, so she could not very well refuse.

I knew I had not been in the right with Mamma, and I thought that maybe I am just a wicked little girl. I began to wonder if my secret writing might be wrong, though it is such a relief and pleasure to me. Then I thought, a relief? But I am always afraid I will be found out!

And suddenly, I knew, Feo, that you would tell me that I ought to explain at least some part of my dilemma to Lehzen. She was sitting there working on her embroidery and looking at me very curiously from time to time, and it smote my heart to think I might cause her more worry by being so wicked. So, before Mr. Davys came back to us, I said to her, "Dear Baroness, there is something I want to talk to you about before luncheon. I mean, <u>privately</u>." And she said, "Of course, my princess."

Toire came in and took the tape measure and went away.

Then the Reverend Mr. Davys came back, and we started in on the Hundred Years War, 1337 until 1453. I asked him why it is not the Hundred and Sixteen Years War, and he looked over the top of his spectacles at me and said, "Your Highness, don't you think a hundred sufficient?"

7 JUNE

Now I must continue my story.

By and by, on the day of the unfortunate incident with Mamma, Mrs. Anderson arrived to give me my singing lesson, and we all went into the music room. We sang "'Twas a Nightingale" until I wanted to throttle the thing and have it in a pie for luncheon. So I sang it once through, "'Twas a Topping Gale," and Mrs. Anderson gave me a puzzled look, but as I didn't do it again during the lesson, she made no remark on it.

Then came my piano teacher, Mr. Sales, and I practiced

my scales. I cannot span a whole octave on the keyboard yet, but he says he has no doubt my hands will be large enough by the time I am a young lady of fourteen. It seems a long time to wait.

Then, Toire being at last downstairs working at French-sewing, Lehzen and I set about playing dolls until luncheon time. I was making Prince Henry the Navigator and the Black Prince. Lehzen was making a shield of papier-mâché for the Black Prince.

I said to her, "Baroness Lehzen, I wish to confide to you a problem I am suffering."

She behaved in a casual manner. She said she hoped she could be helpful. So, _very_ quietly I told her I had hidden something in that drawing room.

Lehzen continued for a moment to look at her gluey layers of parcel paper. I was putting bits of red tinsel on a nice bit of brass the clockmaker replaced and gave me when he repaired Uncle Sussex's library clock. It looks a good deal like a crown and is fortunately the right size for Prince Henry's peg-doll head to jam into it tight so it doesn't come off. It does make the Prince too top-heavy to stand by himself, though, unless his feet are set in the peg-board.

"Is it some sort of . . . pet?" she asked me first. (You see, she does remember your dormouse in the cushion, Feo.) Then she asked how I'd happened to go upstairs unattended. I feared answering because I still did not know what she would do about it. But one cannot lie.

"Oh, you know," I said, "sometimes one is as good as invisible. I was not unattended, I was only quick. I ran ahead when Fanny chased her ball into the drawing room this morning." And that was the truth.

Then she asked if what I'd hidden was something valuable. I assured her it is only important to me, but to me, it is beyond value. And I admitted I am afraid that if Toire were to find it, it would become the property of a Certain Person whose purposes are sometimes unkind. She knew I meant O'Hum.

She said she cannot hide anything for me. I said, "I can manage that part." But if I did not have to be invisible to her as well as everyone else, it would be easier.

I think, really, what with my remarks about invisibility, that she had begun to think I was playacting. So I suddenly resolved to say all and seek her aid. I whispered to her that it was my diary that I hid. As I said the words, I was overcome with fear, for the thought of doing without my journal made me feel, all at once, empty and choked with feelings.

I thought her expression looked alarmed, yet her voice stayed calm, and she looked directly into my eyes. "It is, perhaps, a sort of — schedule?" she suggested. "Rather," I said, but it did not seem entirely truthful. "Also memoranda about my lessons, and thoughts about my soul, and what we have for dinner. That sort of thing."

I told her I <u>like</u> to write because it makes my boring days seem more interesting. And then, I don't lose track of my lessons, who wins or who loses the Hundred Years War, or who dances with whom. I told her I believe it is a useful habit.

Well, she said at first, she never thought it prudent to keep a journal. At that, I put my hand on her arm and begged. "Lehzen," I said, "it is my only privacy. Surely it is my right, if I chuse to have it."

For the longest moment in the history of the world, she waved the shield in the air to dry it. Then, finally, she smiled a bit. "This is England, not Hanover," she said.

Then she became quite firm, and said I must show her how I manage to be invisible. I was so relieved that she was not angry and will not betray my secret, I suppose, I expect what I said sounded rather saucy. "Sometimes I fly up the stairs so swiftly as to be unseen," I said, "while you are in the water closet, thinking invisible thoughts yourself."

"Indeed, Your Highness!" was all she could say to that, because de Spaeth came in.

Then we went down for luncheon. Let me try to recall: We had turbot with lobster sauce, I think, and saddle of lamb, besides a *mayonnaise* of macaroni, lettuces in vinegar and salt, and peas in cream, and cheesecake with woodland strawberries from Devon. Mamma ate a little lamb, and peas and dessert. And she would not have cider, but only a glass of white spring wine. I told Mamma again that I was sorry and kissed her hand, and she kissed my forehead. I ate two helpings of everything.

What one's meals are like will make a difference to what sort of day it turns out to be.

O'Hum did not dine with us, being out purchasing a good whip for the horses for the drive to Claremont.

12 JUNE

Aunt Soap is distressed. At dinner she told Uncle Sussex that the Lord Chamberlain and Lady Conyngham have been permitting His Majesty's physicians to give him too much laudanum, and, though it quiets the pain, it disagrees with him. Alas, now I wonder if that is why his eyes were so bright when he was speaking to me at the ball. I worry at this frailty in His Majesty. Truly, a heavy sword hangs over the head that wears the Crown. But everyone expects him to bear up, after all.

Uncle Billy has gout in his hands, so badly he says it's as if there are pebbles inside his fingers, and he can't hold reins. But he, I am sure, takes no such medicines.

LATER

Things are more settled down now. It is evening, the air fresh and blue outside the window, over the gardens and Hyde Park. I am sitting by the window writing, Lehzen is keeping guard, and my Duke Papa's old tortoiseshell watch ticks endlessly. Mamma is so good at keeping it wound just right.

I must confess, I have been reluctant to let Lehzen immediately see the secret diary-hiding places I have discovered so far. At least, I haven't fetched it when I thought for certain that she would see me.

Since the morning I told Lehzen about my diary, she has made only one further remark. When I finally showed it to her (I mean, the cover of it — she has vowed she does not wish to read what's in it) she said, "My princess, allow me to suggest — as well as being free to claim privacy, Your Highness should never forget: Should any individual's further service merit you overlooking certain faults, you are free to erase. Even the truth. This you should not regard necessarily as dishonesty; it may be only discretion."

I did not point out that I generally write in ink.

13 June

Strawberries and cream at breakfast.
Strawberries and cream at luncheon.
Strawberries and cream at dinner.
A perfect day.

17 JUNE

Oh, fie, what dismal news. My Uncle Cumberland has decided he ought to stay here in England the whole year-round.

Now, I suppose, any time I am lucky enough to be invited to Windsor, I shall have to see Georgie, so it will be a great deal less lucky, should it happen.

22 JUNE

Great, extreme, considerable, enormous HAPPINESS! We shall be going to Claremont to stay with Uncle Leopold for several weeks, and thence to Ramsgate for a lovely, long holiday by the sea! I am _very_ VERY greatly, extremely, considerably, enormously JOYFUL!

De Spaeth helped me put new sky blue ribbons on my straw sunbonnet. She is coming with us, as Mamma can't do without her for long; but she is to return home to Kensington from Ramsgate somewhat before the rest of us. They will have finished the bedrooms and the hallways nearest our apartments by then, and she will make certain things are as they ought to be.

2 July
CLAREMONT

Dear Feo, if only you were here with us, my happiness would be entire! We arrived at midafternoon, quite hot and dusty from the ride (and if we were anywhere else, I'm sure I would have been an unpleasant companion!). But Claremont is my favourite place on all the earth. (And Ramsgate, as well, except it is so hot there. But really, wherever Uncle Leopold is, that is my favourite place.)

Scarcely had Uncle embraced us and offered us cool drinks, than O'Hum told Mamma she should go and lie down to recover from the exertion of so much of the day spent in travel. He went out to the stable to see to the horses. (He is certain Uncle Leopold's stable men need more overseeing than they are likely to get.) So he was out of the way for the rest of the afternoon!

When Lehzen and Mrs. MacLeod had set the chambermaid to unpacking our trunks and satchels, we changed our travel clothes for light muslin frocks. I put my doll Katherine on my pillow, and we went down to join Uncle. We all sipped lemon squash, and he assured me the hoops and the butterfly nets are just where we left them in the little green shed. Mr. Mackintosh, the gardener, can fetch them whenever they're wanted. Now I am in Paradise.

Mamma came down at teatime, and she and Lehzen and Uncle gossiped. Mamma seemed almost carefree. Mrs. Louis came in from her housekeeping duties, and Uncle invited her to sit with us for a bit, but she does not like to presume above her station. She just wanted to make sure we will tell her if anything can be improved with regard to the maids or the meals or the staff. She curtsied to me just as to Mamma and Uncle, a very deep, old-fashioned dip, right down on her knee. Then she said to Uncle, with <u>tears</u> in her eyes, "Please to excuse me, Your Royal Highness, but the princess is so like our other Princess." She was so devoted to Princess Charlotte.

Besides lemon squash and Darjeeling tea — I was permitted one cup, with lump sugar — we had a summer pudding of five kinds of berries plus peaches, and biscuits shaped like seashells.

In the cool evening, Lehzen and I took hoops into the garden and ran them along the paths. It is no wonder they say Heaven smells of roses and lilies.

Afterward, we were sitting on a stone bench, rather panting, and I said, "Is it not <u>glorious</u>, dear Lehzen?" She said, rather slowly, "I fear I have been so lenient with Your Highness of late, you will never again regard me with proper awe." But I assured her I am <u>most</u> in awe of wisdom and learning, not so much of strictness. And I will forever be grateful for her trust.

5 JULY

If I could live here at Claremont forever, Feo, I would. It is so different from ordinary life, it's like dancing instead of trudging.

7 JULY

Went to church at St. George in Esher. After the service, we knelt and said a prayer by the pretty marble monument to my Aunt Princess Charlotte. Uncle held my hand as we came out into the sunshine.

These lovely evenings! Uncle and Lehzen and I make such wonderful conversation, just as if I am grown up. And, most times, Dr. Stockmar speaks with me as well. Stocky is so quiet and gentle, and of course, so highly intelligent — very scientific, I must say. He knows chemistry and geology as well as the usual things. He always seems to me the ideal friend of our dear Uncle, Feo. (He told me I may call him "Stocky" because it was Aunt Charlotte's name for him. He calls her "Your Aunt-Cousin-Princess Lottie.") Even Mamma, when O'Hum is not about, engages in discussion with great interest, and makes witty comments, and <u>laughs</u>.

Fortunately, O'Hum usually writes letters in his room in the evening, or in the study, when Mamma has correspondence to dictate to him. I think he stays there because he becomes so impatient with Uncle Leopold's step-by-step way of coming to a point. And he becomes so annoyed with Stocky's soft voice and his dry sense of humor, which I think O'Hum does not like to show that he does not always understand. (I don't always, myself, but that does not bother me. Sometimes Lehzen explains it to me afterward. She does not miss anything.)

9 JULY

Uncle has a most curious little toy. He calls it his "drizzler." It is a little boxy machinery thing that undoes the gold and silver embroidery from old laces and epaulets, and makes little nests of golden and silver thread, fine as silk floss. I asked Uncle if he would give me a little of it, it was so pretty. He gave me a bit of the silver, but he said I should be patient, and he will save up the gold he drizzles each evening as we sit talking, and get me a more worthy present when he has accumulated more of it.

I said, "I had <u>thought</u> the old lace on the officers' jackets was mere <u>decoration</u>. Now I see that gold lace is — gold. But perhaps, if each of His Majesty's officers had a little drizzling machine, then sometime, if their poor troops needed supplies on some foreign strand, they might undo all their epaulets and be able to buy what they wanted from the natives."

"An excellent plan," Stocky said. Somehow, though, the look he exchanged with Uncle made me think they only found my idea amusing. But I still think it would be prudent if every regiment and every ship of the line carried a drizzler along, in case some emergency should arise.

11 JULY

An exceptionally rainy day. Uncle and Lehzen and de Spaeth and Stocky and Lord Craven, who came visiting, and I read Shakespeare aloud together, *The Tempest.* Uncle was Prospero, I was Miranda, Lehzen was Ariel, Stocky was Caliban, and Lord Craven and de Spaeth did everybody else. It was simply <u>wonderful</u>! Lehzen and Stocky have the most ability, for they changed their voices admirably, and Lehzen seemed already to know her lines.

Mamma was indisposed after staying up late last night. O'Hum was writing letters and otherwise occupied. I believe he has found a way to get the bay mares, after all, but it seems to involve his going here and there and doing a lot of visiting with Mr. Owen and some other gentlemen.

12 JULY

Rain again. Played twelve games of bell and hammer. In desperation, I believe, Uncle has promised to teach me chess.

13 JULY

Uncle had to be away today. It was overcast, though not raining (for the most part).

Sketched Lehzen and Mrs. Louis and the chambermaid (as a dairy maid).

Played three games of bell and hammer with Lehzen and Mamma. In the second one, my dice came up blank at <u>every single throw</u>. They agreed they had never seen such a thing.

14 JULY

Sunday at St. George's again. A wasp was buzzing all around us in the pews for about a quarter of an hour. I sat very still and prayed it would not sting anyone, and the Lord heard my prayer. But I don't know if that is a miracle or only good luck. In fact, I don't know if one may call anything "luck" that happens in church. I shall try to remember to ask the Reverend Mr. Davys.

There was veal at dinner, but for some reason I kept thinking, <u>Diamond, heifer of Rose; Irene, heifer of Rose,</u> so I declined the schnitzel. Instead, I had a Cornish hen with sauce of raspberries, and potatoes mashed and fluffed into little swirled domes like a Russian palace and broiled golden-brown. Uncle's Cook does such things most beautifully.

16 JULY

O'Hum on a tear, raging at Mamma over something when they came in from visiting. Lehzen took me out into the garden.

20 JULY

Oh, Feo, the MOST TERRIBLE POSSIBILITY. It is simply unbearable! Uncle Leopold has been invited to go to <u>Greece</u> and be King there. He told me it may happen, but he must consider whether it would be a wise choice.

I am afraid I wept piteously and begged him not to go away. He patted my hand and kissed my cheek and pressed my hand to his heart and said it would be many months before he can decide.

Later, Mamma and Lehzen told me I must bear up, because the fate of nations hangs on his reply.

And here is something odd. O'Hum seemed almost as distressed as I — though, I must say, for different reasons. He said, "You see, he has always had his own objective, his own best interests, most before him. He is not a thoroughly dependable ally." Mamma was curt to him, and only said, "You are wrong, you will see."

MOST miserable.

I had an odd dream — really, almost more like a memory.

In it, I was a tiny child again, and it was the time Grandmamma Coburg was visiting here at Claremont, and she had brought our cousins Ernest and Albert with her — remember, Feo? And in this dream, I was riding on the back of my little white donkey, Blanco, that Uncle York gave me before he passed away. I wanted to climb down and run and play with Albert on a hillside covered with white flowers, as thick as a snowy white fleece, and I could see Uncle Leopold and Stocky were strolling nearby, too. But I was too small to get down and run to them. Blanco's little bells kept jingling, jingling. Then, Captain Conroy came to me and lifted me down, so gently, he was quite like Uncle York.

I woke up then, and I was weeping. My Papa is dead, and Uncle York is, too, and I shan't see them again until we meet in heaven. Everyone says Uncle King will die soon, too. And Uncle Leopold may go to live far away. I wish O'Hum would be kind to me.

Lehzen woke up and came and put her arms around me.

LATER

We are all going on holiday to Ramsgate tomorrow. It will take us many days to get there. We must be gracious and stay overnight with so many of Mamma's influential friends all along our route. How tiresome! I am quite eager for the seaside!

Uncle showed me that he is packing his little traveling chess set. He said he is sorry to cause me any sadness, and he repeated that he has not decided whether or not he would like to go to Greece. But he says they have a new constitution, and very many grave problems requiring wise and strong solutions, so it is an honour to be sought out by them. He must give the matter serious consideration.

I did not cry again — not while I was with him.

22 JULY
BLETCHINGLEY

We are traveling to Ramsgate in the Isle of Thanet, Kent. We go by way of Croydon, Bromley, Strood, Rochester, Chatham, Faversham, Whitstable, Herne Bay, Reculver, and Margate. We have stopped for refreshment. I cannot write more until we

Now I can finish. I am writing now in the room Lehzen and I share at Lord Stanhop's sister-in-law's house (I hope I have got that right.) Everywhere we stop, I curtsy and say I am pleased to make their acquaintance. Our host and hostess kiss my hand, and talk to Mamma about me over my head as if I am an infant, and Lehzen takes me away to rest. I am extraordinarily well rested. I wish she would take me away to dance or climb a hill or talk to that little Gypsy girl who called to us as we drove past, saying that she would read our fortunes if we gave her silver.

Mamma and O'Hum and Uncle Leopold travel in the high-wheeled phaeton. Uncle and O'Hum, each with their saddle horses along, take it by turns to ride horseback alongside of the carriages most of the time. Mr. Robertson, the groom, rides the other horse. Lehzen and de Spaeth and the Reverend Mr. Davys and I ride in the chariot, and Grampion rides on the box with Mr. Graham. Dr. Stockmar and Mrs. MacLeod and Mrs. Louis roll along in the barouche, and sometimes the Reverend Mr. Davys rides with them so we can nap. But I prefer to look out the window. This land is beautiful, fat, strange, severe, and beautiful again by turns. If the carriage did not jolt so, I would be continually sketching, for there are pleasing prospects so often.

24 JULY
LUDDESDOWN

I asked Lehzen if I may read to myself in the carriage. (I thought she was about to start in on a volume of sermons, which creates rather a drone in our small, hot carriage-parlor, as if there is a large bluebottle fly buzzing in the corner.) Alas, she had foreseen my reluctance, and so, she said I might instead chuse to begin on my Latin.

Truly, I don't know why it is called "going on holiday." I think I would faint if ever I did <u>not</u> have <u>some</u> unpleasant task to accomplish <u>every</u> day.

I would rather read a story.

It is simply impossible to recall all the names of all the persons and places that have been mentioned to me. I am v. tired of travel. I'm sure I don't know why we don't go by boat.

O'Hum fusses so much about harnesses. About everything.

LATER

Rochester is a v. novel city, and the people are v. civil, warm, and pleasant. We were shown around the cathedral by someone, I can't recall his name just now, and I haven't much time to write. Everything was restored, v. lovely, especially a v. old statue of a bishop that had been buried in a wall. It was taken out a few years ago and had its paint touched up.

Coming through Bromley, Lehzen and I took it by turns to read "The Raven" from the Grimms' *Kinder-und-Hausmärchen*. V. good story.

In Strood we saw a chalk quarry. V. interesting.

Everywhere one looked out the window, it was yellow

broom or hops flowers, or, on shadier roads, cherry orchards and little children with baskets of cherries. When we stopped to give the horses water, de Spaeth gave me a sixpence to buy a basket from a little girl. She handed a basket in to us, and I put the coin right into her cherrypink-stained little hand. We ate cherries, then, all the way to the next village.

26 JULY
FAVERSHAM

Oh, upon my word. There are entirely too many Historical Places where someone had his or her head cut off in England, and many of them Royal heads, too. But sometimes an Archbishop. We are near Canterbury.

28 JULY
RAMSGATE

What BLISS! We're here at Uncle Leopold's house at dear, dear East Cliff! Feo, if only you were here with us!

The air and the waters, all so clean and lovely — even the gravel paths white as marble! The privet hedges are all blooming, and there are butterflies everywhere except right along the seafront.

As Lehzen and I started up the stairs to our room, Uncle handed Lehzen a little note that had been left with the housekeeper, closed with a wafer of deep green sealing wax. When we were upstairs, she opened it and read it, then passed it to me, with an expression of great pleasure showing on her dear face. The note said:

Your Highness,
You honour us with your visit to Ramsgate. I
hope you will find opportunity to visit my garden,
as you have been kind enough to do on past happy
occasions. You will find the cool weather last
month has preserved the pink roses here at East
Cliff. So that you may come and go freely, I am
enclosing the key to the gate near the topiary
giraffe.

Your obedient servant,
M. Montefiore

And there, indeed, was a little golden key, with a long loop of green satin ribbon through it, so I can wear it like a necklace and not lose it.

30 JULY

Weather v. HOT. To the seaside all yesterday afternoon. I begged to be allowed to engage a donkey-drawn bathing machine to be pulled through the water, for I should like to learn how to swim. However, Lehzen would not hear of it. So I waded barefoot in the soft, green, crystal waves.

Mamma came down and walked along with me, picking up bits of pretty coloured sea ferns to mount on blotting paper. I have started a shell collection. I will bring some particularly nice ones to Toire, who is with her mother and sister, Jane, this month.

But really, I don't see why <u>she</u> has holidays <u>away</u> from O'Hum and I <u>don't</u>.

1 August

Went out early (before breakfast) with Lehzen and Uncle Leopold to Mr. Montefiore's garden. We saw there not only the good old giraffe carved out of a bush, but this year a bear (standing up, dancing) and a great swan, as well. Dew lay on the roses, lovely indeed. Also on the bed of lady's mantle, where the drops run down to the center of each round, green, flannel leaf to make a little jewel, like a drop of quicksilver. It was all magical and fairylike.

Uncle says he cannot tell if he believes in fairies, as he does not think of them often enough to form an opinion.

2 August

Going along the shore with Mamma, Baroness de Spaeth, Baroness Lehzen, Lord Albemarle (he is here visiting some friends at Lord Granville's), and Captain Conroy:

O'Hum: *Hot as Gibraltar, what!*

Mamma: *Do hold your parasol up, Vickelchen.*

Lehzen: *Watch, now, that your skirt doesn't get wet!*

Lord Albemarle: *Pray, allow me to assist you to remove your little slippers. Barefoot's the thing!*

De Spaeth: *Your bonnet will do you no good, tipped back so far.*

O'Hum: *Burn you to a blackamoor! Blisters on your nose! Skin peels right off!*

Mamma: *Do hold your parasol up, Vickelchen!*

How irksome I find all this attention!

V. tired after luncheon.

I miss you, Feo.

4 AUGUST

Only an hour of lessons. I am afraid I was distracted. O'Hum was annoyed with someone — I didn't hear it all. Mamma closed the door.

5 AUGUST

Uncle and Dr. Stockmar have begun to teach me chess. I have learned how the pieces move. Even the castles move — Uncle says they are more like siege towers on

wheels, or elephants with archers on their backs. I said,
"Perhaps they are called 'rooks' because rooks are big, but
they can fly."

6 August

Fried fish at breakfast, scrambled eggs, thick toast, crisp
on the outside, with lime curd, soft, fresh cheese, v. white
and shining. The fish was caught last night and could not
have been better.

Walked along the sea with the Reverend Mr. Davys.
Should not do this if I am unwilling to discuss Saints
Peter, Andrew, James, or John, or Jonah. Wanted desper-
ately to dig in the sand.

I declare, everyone takes their holidays hereabout, if
they don't go to Brighton. Uncle King used to go to
Brighton. I wonder if he has gone this season, or if he has
been too ill.

7 August

Uncle and Stocky and Lehzen and I went to Mr. Montefiore's house for tea and chess. Mr. M. has a lovely set carved of olive wood from the Holy Land. He says that in Italy, the pawns are called labourer, blacksmith, weaver, merchant, physician, innkeeper, tax-collector, and gambler.

Stocky and Mr. M. were v. funny. Uncle had taken a good number of my pieces and had me checked. I said, "Is it 'mate,' then? Have I lost the game?"

Stocky said, "Can't have that — what if this enemy were truly wicked, eh?"

I said, "But I see no move!"

Then Mr. Montefiore said, "A good time to turn the table on him!" And, indeed, he turned the table, rotating the chessboard a quarter turn. Looking at it that way, the positions of the black and white squares were different. I had a choice of several new moves — and I very handily took my king out of check!

I did not wish to win dishonourably. "Is that fair play?" I asked Uncle Leopold. He patted my hand, smiled, and said, "It is history, my dear. Our friends want us to remember that in real life, one's moves are not simply black or white."

I shall have to think about this.

8 August

Beautiful, beautiful day. Little time to write. Perhaps later.

9 August

Yesterday, walked along the sands all the way to Broadstairs with Uncle, Stocky, Lehzen, and Grampion. We engaged a charming donkey cart to carry our luncheon basket and my paint box and sketchbook, and sometimes Lehzen rode, but I hardly did at all. Grampion forgot to ask the donkey's name, so we called it Nick Bottom. The cart was purple, and it had scarlet poppies painted on it, v. pretty. I painted a picture of it, using seawater.

I took a good deal of sun. Today my arms and hands and the tops of my feet are quite red, but I don't say they sting, for it is my own fault. De Spaeth gave me a little jar of almond salve and it is v. soothing.

Mamma was indisposed at dinnertime.

10 AUGUST

Went out in a lovely boat. O'Hum got sick over the rail. I felt fine, excepting only that going to the carriage afterward was odd and giddy. I asked Lehzen if I had begun to walk as Uncle Billy does, rolling from side to side. I fear she thought I was being too pert.

12 AUGUST

Uncle King's birthday. He is sixty-seven years old. We were awakened this morning by guns firing a salute in the harbour. We are to go to a reception this evening with addresses, musical tributes, a collation, and fireworks. Mamma and O'Hum are turning themselves inside out to find things to say that uphold the Throne and the Royal Family without sounding as if His Majesty has much to do with it.

I remarked on this to Uncle Leopold. He said, "Your Mamma's position is politically delicate. But you know how the knight moves, my dear. With every advance, he must decide upon which side of his horse it's safest to dismount."

In a chess game, of course, the knight goes two squares in one direction, then another square to either side. I believe Uncle meant Sir John Conroy, whom my Uncle King made a knight, is not always straightforward.

If I had my pearl necklace with me, I would wear it. However, it is back in Kensington. I hope Mamma and Lehzen will allow me to stay up late for the fireworks.

13 AUGUST

Fireworks were quite dazzling, but v. loud.

Best of the refreshments were the cherry ices.

May my Uncle King enjoy many more happy returns of this day. I should not like having Uncle Ernest as King. Uncle Billy would be better. Mamma does not like either of them very well, I'm afraid.

17 AUGUST

You'll never guess, Feo, what O'Hum got Mamma for her birthday!

ANOTHER PUPPY! He is a DARLING! SWEET! CLEVER! He is a golden tan-and-white King Charles spaniel. His coat is v. curly and is like SILK. He has a little pug face and dainty ears. Mamma named him Dash, because he does. He already knows his name, and looks up when he is called, and sometimes will come to me when I summon him.

De Spaeth is going to take him back with her to the palace when she goes, so we need not have him where it is so hot.

Mamma had remarked how she wished she could see the Tyrolean Alps again some year. I cannot pay for such a trip abroad with my pocket money, as I would like to be able to do as my birthday present to her. Before we left home, though, I already painted her a picture of Tyrolean girls, and I have had it with me in my bandbox. I used as my model the peg-doll Lehzen and I dressed for my geography lesson last February, and used Fanny as the model for their dog, only made her sandy-coloured (but, alas, too small).

I also bought her perfume, some *eau Romaine* and some *eau de miel d'Angleterre.* They both smell v. exquisite. I am not sure which she may like better. I hope she will say, by and by.

When I gave my gifts to her, Mamma said, "Thank you, *ma délice.*" She kissed my hair and my two cheeks, and said the faces and hat and the speckled shawl and the eardrops on the standing Tyrol girl are "*très remarquables, très délicats*" — very remarkable and delicate.

25 SEPTEMBER
KENSINGTON PALACE

We are home again, back in plain, old Kensington Palace.

Such a long while since I've written in my journal!

First, I became bilious the afternoon after Mamma's birthday, and Mamma fussed around so I had no privacy. If Stocky had not been around to reassure her that no one had given me a poisoned biscuit, I'm sure I should have had to take all sorts of very nasty physicks and such.

Then O'Hum took his poor horse, Snuff, out on a wet ride, and brought him back lame. That meant he could not ride him on the way back home, and rode in the chariot with us instead. It made the trip v. tedious. He, himself, is the hero of every story he recounts. I was actually glad finally to see the black and gold of the palace gates.

O'Hum is so put out about Snuff, nothing pleases him, and he has decided I am not advanced enough in my lessons, so I am to be allowed less time for play and leisure now. He says I must Put My Back In It. I was v. naughty. I pretended innocence and said, "Is that what's wrong with Snuff, he didn't put his back in it?" He was v. irritated and gave me a lecture on horsemanship. I did not point out I am not the one who lamed my horse.

I must tell about Fanny and Dash, but no

27 SEPTEMBER

I meant to say, no time now. But there really was NO time. I miss my writing, but I fear there's no help for it. I shan't be permitted more leisure to do as I like.

About my darling little dogs: When de Spaeth arrived back here, the painters and plasterers had done all, but Cook and the staff were in a pother because poor little Dash had been staying down in the kitchen while the work was carried out, and he ate some RAT POISON! He almost DIED! He lay about and stared and panted and drooled horridly, and everyone thought he was done for.

Of course, they knew Mamma and I would be ever so sad.

When I returned, all my care was for our poor little friend. Mamma would not let me have him upstairs at first, but gave in rather than have me always down in the kitchen. They all say now that he has only recovered because I nursed him myself, and they are sure he would have died if I had not come home when I did. Now he has quite recovered, except his back legs sometimes tremble for no reason. I cannot see that he ought to be turned into a hunting dog, as O'Hum seems to have intended. I am happy to say Mamma agrees with me.

At first Fanny was jealous of Dash for all the attention he received, but now she treats him as if he is her puppy and she is his mother. She likes to lick his ears. It is comical to watch.

1 OCTOBER

Lehzen and I costumed two new dolls, one as the singer Maria Malibran in her role as Mathilde in *William Tell*, and the other as Lady Durham dressed for the opera. We have started a list of all the dolls we've dressed so far. There are forty-six of them. I don't count the first four, for they are so untidy now, I show them to no one. I was only learning to sew then — my stitches were but three to the inch.

8 OCTOBER

O'Hum's birthday this month. I cannot think what I ought to do for a gift. For my birthday, he and Mamma gave me my red plush saddle for Rosa. But I haven't enough money to do so much.

9 OCTOBER

I have had an idea. I am painting a portrait of Victoire for O'Hum's gift. Mr. Westall says I do a nice likeness when I set my mind to it. Toire sits v. still, and when she wants to make a remark, she whispers, as if her face will not move so much if she does not speak normally. She says, "Are my eyes open wide enough? I don't wish to appear drowsy. But perhaps it is more effective to look dreamy and thoughtful. Does my hair appear smooth? The weather is so damp today, I'm sure it could not be as sleek as it ought to be. Oh, do make my frock blue! Yellow is not my best colour."

I wonder if she's ever been told that a picture is better than a thousand words.

10 OCTOBER

I fear I have become impatient with my painting, as well as with Toire. I recall our visit to the British Museum to see Lord Elgin's collection of Greek sculpture from the Parthenon of Athens. Now I feel painting is a poor, flat thing compared to statues. If I were a real artist, I'm sure I should learn to sculpt.

And to think that Uncle Leopold might undertake to govern Greece, so rich in classic art. Yet I cannot bear the thought of his going away.

Oh, Feo, how can such things come about? What did we ever do, to deserve such bitter pain? Life will never be sweet, never. I hate Captain Conroy. It is only today that it has become calm again. But it is a terrible calm, like a church after a funeral.

Captain Conroy's birthday — oh, fie on the day. Mamma gave him one of my Duke Papa's field watches as a gift, and I wish she had not done it. She said it was because he was so devoted to Papa and shared her memories of him better than others do. I thought that was unfair, for I can't help not remembering, and I'm sure my Papa's own brothers and sisters remember him as well as Captain Conroy does, probably better. But she as good as admitted he told her himself he'd like to have it, and, as she said, she could not very well turn down a request that revealed such loyalty and devotion.

I gave him the picture I painted (as well as some tobacco in a very handsome tin I bought with my own pocket money). Toire and I stood there while he inspected it, and he said, "Oh, hmm, very nice, very nice indeed. Tell Westall he's done a good job on you, Your Highness. You've a great deal of talent, not all little girls do." But he didn't say it was pretty, and Toire was let down.

I would feel more sympathy toward her if she had not been so grumpose to me all day afterward. It was not my fault and I did make her frock blue and even put blond lace on the sleeves, which came out well.

There is just something about O'Hum's sensibility to gifts. Toire gave him *savon bergamot*, a pleasant, manly soap. Uncle Sussex recommended it, and it was a v. nice choice, I would have thought. O'Hum said, "Oh, hmm, thank you, m'girl," nary a word more.

A great many guests came to dinner. He had to hold forth — every opinion of his own was awesome for cleverness, and no one else had information he would admit was correct, but he was entirely wise about everything, and he would explain why. It was all his especial friends and people for whom he does favours. They all drank a great deal of wine and said, "He's a capital fellow." Someone I overheard but did not see, for he was behind the Chinese screen — and I am glad not to know who is such a traitor — said, "If only Sir John had the management of the Throne, he'd whip it all into shape, would he not?"

Feo, this makes me ill, remembering.

LATER

Mamma was having a pleasant evening at first, I believe. There was pheasant and saddle of venison and crown roast of pork and a great lot of other stuff, everything O'Hum likes, and six wines. When Mrs. MacLeod took Toire, and Lehzen and I went up to bed, Mamma was full of cheer and had roses on her cheeks.

I went to sleep for quite a while, I thought, but something woke me v. late at night. I'd taken a nap in the afternoon because of the party, so I was all at once v. much awake, not at all sleepy. So I thought I'd write, since I have so little time for it these days. I had put my diary in the red drawing room behind the inlaid cabinet full of little ivory elephants that General Clive brought home from India, and I crept out of bed to go and get it. Lehzen must have been deep asleep, for she said nothing to me. And she does snore a bit, not loudly, but one can hear her.

I was halfway down to the corner of the corridor when I heard Captain Conroy's voice up ahead, and I saw there was a crack of light around the door into the card room. I thought at first that he'd stayed up playing whist and was arguing over the game.

"What SHE likes, is it?" he was saying. "NEVER a

woman who knew what she liked nor would shut her mouth blathering about what SHE likes, what SHE likes!"

Then — oh, Feo, I heard Mamma's voice, and she did <u>not</u> sound calm.

"Lower your tone," she said. "Don't talk to me so." But she did not sound firm. There was a different quality in her voice. I think she was distressed and agitated.

I came close to the door, thinking I would fling it open and say they would cause me a bad dream. But as I approached, I heard some piece of furniture scraping suddenly across the floor, and Captain Conroy saying, lower, but very angrily, "Always what SHE likes, but who does the work, I ask you!" Then I heard more scraping, and a thump against the wall.

I thought Mamma might not like me to intrude on a private quarrel, but this did not seem usual. So, although I was terrified, I stepped up to the door and peered into the room.

Oh, Feo. He had her pushed against the wall in the corner, and was holding her there. She twisted and tried to escape him, but he held her fast against the paneling, and kept saying, "SHE wants, does she, does she? But who's the one who does the work, eh?"

I could tell he might harm her. I was sure of it.

But here is the problem: I didn't know if he meant what <u>Mamma</u> wants, or what <u>I</u> want. For they are both always looking out for my interests, they are always telling me. So I thought if I went in, he might turn on me, too, and Mamma would be worse off.

I was such a coward. I am ashamed of it now. I am not like my Papa. I ran back down the corridor to Mamma's antechamber. De Spaeth was there, sitting up reading, waiting for Mamma to turn in. I was trembling and weeping (I realized later) and could hardly speak sensibly, but waved my arm, pointing, and said, "He's hurting her, stop him hurting her!" And de Spaeth leapt up from her chair and said, "An assassin, a robber?"

"The Captain!" I told her. "Sir John!"

But de Spaeth did not seem to understand me. At least, I thought, either she didn't understand or she just didn't believe me. She said, "Your Highness, you should be in bed!"

I said, "A good thing I'm not! The Captain is attacking Mamma! Stop him!" But she seized me by the hand and brought me into my corner of the bedchamber and tucked me in (so tight I could scarcely breathe) before she went to help Mamma, and I was furious at her. She is not a good hand in an emergency! I would never have thought it of her, but she was <u>slow</u>, Feo! If I had been Uncle Billy, I would have been roaring at her, "<u>Put on more canvas, by God!</u>" Had it been an <u>assassin</u>, Mamma would have been murdered by that time!

But that is only the first part of the terrible story, and now I must go to sleep. I will try to write the rest tomorrow, for the world is upside down.

1 NOVEMBER

The sadness drags on.

I meant to stay awake until I heard Mamma come in to her end of our suite. But, abed, in the darkness, I could not tell when I drifted off.

In the morning, Lehzen had to wake me up for breakfast. Mamma was indisposed and so was de Spaeth, I thought. The Captain had gone out to the country shooting with Count Zichy's equerry at someone's private park. It turned out later that, besides my Papa's watch, Mamma had given him a weimaraner bird dog we are not to be permitted to spoil.

Before my lessons, I went to Mamma's door with a posy of asters and chrysanthemums I picked while Lehzen and I gave Fanny and Dash their exercise. I thought it likely she was awake, but she was not. Mrs. MacLeod said she and de Spaeth sat up talking about old times until dawn and were just going to bed when she came up to supervise the maid, Lutie, who was stirring up the fires.

Everything seemed so natural and slow, I was like to doubt it all — some sort of nightmare no one else recalled.

Only, Lehzen seemed distracted, and excused herself from the room while Mr. Westall had Toire and me sketching seashells, in the style of his father's South Sea Islands pictures. My palm trees appear too flat, for I do not do them from life.

Then Mamma was at luncheon but de Spaeth was not, and when I asked why, Mamma said, "I think you <u>know</u>." But I did not.

Aunt Soap made several attempts to gossip about the dinner party, but Mamma pleaded her headache and did not take up the conversation. So eventually Aunt Soap withdrew to go visit Uncle Sussex, and Mamma told me to go with her and read some *Aesop*. Mamma also said to send Lehzen to her while I was in the library.

Aunt Soap said, "Go over by the globes, there's a good child," so she could tell Uncle Sussex what she had in a note from Aunt Adelaide. When they don't tell me all they have heard about Aunt Adelaide and I know they are speaking of her, I always wonder if she has had another unfortunate infant. It is not fair all her children should have died, for she and Uncle Billy <u>like</u> having little children about. Uncle says, "Well, it keeps one young to bide with young ones whenever one can, for one can't always, after all."

But Aunt waited to get into the letter until I was at the table by the globes, where I could not hear.

I wonder if I am turning into the sort of person Toire is, eavesdropping and tattling on what I think is wrongdoing.

LATER

It is a good thing it's shooting season. The Captain goes out hunting, and I am free to write. Lehzen is terrified, though, and I will explain why, if I can only write a bit longer today.

I did not suspect what a change in our life was already coming about! How bitter, now, my self-blame!

When I returned to the white parlour, there were Lehzen and de Spaeth, sitting, prim and correct, on the pink satin chairs, and de Spaeth said, "Your Highness, you will envy me when I tell you where I am going."

"Where?" I said, thinking she must mean to some performance that evening or for a weekend party at one of the pretty places we'd stayed at in our recent travels.

"Hohenlohe," she said then, in a very quiet and decisive voice. "To Princess Feodora. She will have use for my training when she has a baby."

I could not believe what I was hearing! Kensington Palace has always had dear de Spaeth here for Mamma! I looked at her more closely and could not see that she had been weeping. But she does not get little purple speckles under her eyes as Aunt Soap does from the exertion of tears, and besides, she is v. deft with cosmetics when she <u>chuses</u> to be. But even so, I thought she <u>had</u> been weeping. How could she not? She has been Mamma's lady-in-waiting since Mamma was married to <u>your</u> father, Feo! We are her life! I am sure she thought England had become her home! I know she will be glad to be with you, but Mamma is her best friend — or was.

Then the horror of the situation truly struck me, for I

saw that not only was the dear Baroness to go — it was not even something she would choose for herself. Surely, she has been ordered away.

And this is why Lehzen is so nervous. If de Spaeth can be sent away, who's been here <u>forever</u>, WHAT ABOUT LEHZEN?

I must be very, <u>very</u> careful.

I hope Uncle Leopold will come visit us v. SOON.

2 NOVEMBER

The saddest of mornings. It is my Papa's birthday, and dear Baroness de Spaeth has gone. She did not even oversee her own packing, and has taken only her traveling bags and trunk. Mrs. MacLeod will see to the rest. It is so unkind — no, it is more than unkind. It is cruel.

De Spaeth and I had not been alone together this whole time, so I was not able to ask her what she said to Mamma that night. I do not know if Mamma knows it was I who sent the Baroness in to the card room. I tried to speak with Mamma yesterday, and then again this morning. She is v. stiff and distracted with me.

I asked her, "Without our de Spaeth, who will take care of you?" She said that she has other ladies — as if she were saying she has other bonnets.

I told her I would not stand for her being hurt! I looked her in the eye when I said it, so she'd know I know how Captain Conroy treats her.

"The Baroness is not my mother, Vickelchen," she said coldly. "After twenty-five years, she sometimes forgets that. And Lehzen is not your mamma. You obey her because you would obey me. That is all."

I did not like this talk. Mamma seemed to be bending away from all that has happened, erasing and rewriting so it agrees with her better — so it will agree with Captain Conroy. Everything has to agree with him. I hate him.

However, what she was saying about Lehzen made me think twice before saying more. I gave her a very cold, hard look, though, and I did not walk away. I insisted that she should not send de Spaeth away, that it is a very, VERY bad idea.

I thought perhaps she was reconsidering, for it was a long moment before she spoke again. But then she said, "You and everyone else will think I sent her away. Let them think it. She was very improper in a particular way she spoke to me recently. She has gone too far. I cannot tolerate such intrusion and such selfishness from one of my ladies. But I did not cast her off."

"Then you should stop <u>him</u> from doing so," I told her.

"Is that what you think? You are still so young," Mamma said then, and her tone was not entirely gentle. "De Spaeth saw it was time for her to leave, and she has gone. If your father had lived through our first year here, she would have gone back to Germany before this, child. Your father would not have permitted her to be so outspoken. But I had only known him a little when we married, and I did not live in England for even a year before he died. If it had not been for Sir John, we should none of us have done well. You should remember that and learn to be grateful to those who want the best for you."

"I am grateful to the Baroness," I said. "I had thought it a lesson you meant to teach me by example."

Then I curtsied. I did not ask to be excused, but I left her there. I was <u>very</u> angry, and feared if I did not go, I would say things I should be sorry for later.

Riding with Lehzen, Grampion, Lady Cowper. Happened to encounter Aunt Adelaide with Lord Paget and Georgie Cumberland, and Aunt's footman, Tomthorne. We rode two and two, Aunt and Lady Cowper, Lord Paget and Lehzen, Georgie and myself, and Grampion and Tomthorne.

Georgie says our Uncle King will die soon. They all speak of it at Windsor and do not even whisper, he says, for His Majesty does not hear or see well or much care anymore. Except that now everyone must tell him all the time how they love his glorious accomplishments.

"And then, it's Sailor Bill of Clarence who will be king. Aunt Adelaide will be Her Majesty the Queen, and I'll be her favourite, because you remind her of her dead baby girl," Georgie said.

I was about out of my mind, he is so horrid!

"You'd make an awful Queen, you would," he went on, knowing none of the grown-ups were listening. "Uncle William's sixty-four years old, he can't last. My father's only fifty-nine. He'll outlast old Admiral Pineapple-head, see if he doesn't."

I didn't say that my Papa was only fifty-three, younger

than the rest, and the healthiest one in the family, and he didn't outlast them. Fate is in Our Lord's hands, as the Reverend Mr. Davys says.

It seems to me, Georgie is the sort who will have a great number of boys wanting to knock him down for what he says. I am surprised his father doesn't do it, he has such a violent temper.

But our talk was ended then, for a band of schoolboys set off a string of Chinese firecrackers nearby. My poor Rosa took fright and sped right off the bridle path and across the grass there, which was still frosty in the shade under the beech trees. Rosa stayed away from the low branches and in the sun. I was glad for the gallop, only Lehzen was quite white in the face when they all caught up with me.

When we got home and I changed out of my riding suit and boots, I found I had a bruise inside my knee where it hooks over the pommel of my sidesaddle.

I told Lehzen all of what Georgie had said about Uncle King and Uncle William. She said he was quite improper to speak so. She said I should remember he is younger than I am, and a naughty boy.

6 November

I miss Baroness de Spaeth.

I deplore my own Mother's behaviour.

I shall never trust Captain Conroy, not ever more.

Lehzen is as nervous as a cat about my writing, and so I must be v. cautious from now on, even more than before.

Mamma is planning a brilliant dinner party for next month. Lehzen and I dressed dolls as ladies to attend. We made up names for them: Apollonia, Countess Delaville; Juno, Duchess of Durham; Rebekah, Duchess of Mountjoy; and Lady Nina Morton. It is a relief to whisper about dolls, rather than real persons. The Countess Delaville, we decided, has been married three times, and she is divinely happy this time, at last. Her husband, the Count, is a very superior individual. The match was also advantageous to her children's prospects.

8 December

Mamma <u>will</u> have a holiday dinner party, although everyone is still so shocked about poor dear de Spaeth, traveling at such a time of year. I can only remember the last party and how terribly it turned out. My stomach churns at the thought it could happen again. If I pay attention to how things go, perhaps I can make sure it stays amusing for everyone so there'll be no trouble.

I wonder if Uncle Leopold will come to dinner. He has been saying little to Mamma these last few months. They are at odds about de Spaeth and about Greece.

I told Toire I had a headache. It was the truth. My head ached from hearing her make a Remark about Uncle Leopold dying his hair black so he will look like the Greek god Jove to the people of Athens.

9 DECEMBER

Mamma's dinner was a great success. We had six Princesses, two Princes, and three Ambassadors. However, not Uncle Leopold.

We had bisque marine with chervil and lemon, salmi of pheasant and grouse, roast beef with mustard sauce, baked apples, and brandy pudding with hard sauce. Also a lot of dishes I did not eat, for they consisted of sprouts, cabbage, kale, and all that I am not fond of. There were no caraway seeds, alas. Seeds are not the fashion.

Captain Conroy did not drink too much, I am happy to say.

29 DECEMBER

The close of the year. Lehzen says I should be keeping a careful record, if a record I am keeping. I think she is correct. She frequently is, because she thinks as well as listens so much of the time while others are speaking.

Christmas dinner at Claremont, thanks be to heaven. It was so jolly. I gave everyone a good gift. I will list them later, if I have time. Here is what they gave me, and I must write letters of thanks:

Feo and Ernest sent me baby house furniture — a whole library with globes and bookcases, a leather arm-chair and oak table, and a tiny Latin dictionary an inch and a half square with a brass clasp.

Charles sent me a toy called a Thaumatrope. When it spins, you see a picture of a parrot go onto the picture of a perch, and the wig flies off a bald man's head, or back onto his head, if you spin it backward. It has a great number of picture pairs that combine in this droll fashion.

Uncle Leopold gave me two more pearls for my necklace, and Uncle Sussex gave me one. Uncle Sussex gave me a volume of poetry, *The Parliament of Fowles* by Geoffrey Chaucer. Uncle Leopold gave me a mechanistical monkey dressed as a Persian magician. The monkey's eyes roll and he waves his wand while a music box in the base plays "Turkish Rondo."

Lehzen gave me many, MANY Juvenile Theatre character sheets to paint, as well as scripts for *The Casket of Gloriana*, also, *The Fairy of the Oak, or Harlequin's Regatta*, and *Beauty and the Beast, as performed by the Royal Coburg Theatre.*

Stocky gave me a clever bank of cast metal, a soldier that shoots a sixpence or a penny at a bear. The bear's mouth and the soldier's jacket are painted red. The soldier reminds me of Charles's toy soldiers, which have my Papa's among them as well as his Papa's. Charles has them with him in Leiningen, I believe. I wish they were only packed away here at Kensington. I should like to play with them sometimes.

Mamma gave me a v. VERY PRETTY Italian wax doll

with REAL hair and eyes that can be opened and closed with a little wire on her back that sticks out through her dress, which is pink silk with rosettes. I am not sure what I should name her.

Mr. Westall gave me a watercolour his father brought back from Australia. It is of a sort of marsupial squirrel, v. darling and quaint. The picture is in a fine little mahogany frame. I know Mr. Westall must treasure his Father's work, and so I am v. moved by this gift.

I gave Mr. Westall three of my best pieces. The sketch of himself is for him to give to his dear sister, who has not been well. The view of Hampstead is for him to keep, because he will be amused when he remembers the day we worked on it. And the painting of Hagar and Ishmael is for him to send to the Bible Society in Auckland. I signed it *Princess Victoria delineavit Kensington Palace.* That means that I drew it. Mr. Westall says the Society will hold a lottery and sell my painting to raise funds for their support. I think that is v. clever.

Later

Wassailers came a-caroling from Esher, and Uncle had them in and gave them rum punch and lamb's wool, which is hot, spiced ale and wine frothed up with mashed apples. They sang six-part harmony on some carols.

We had consommé royale with custard cubes, served up in my Princess Aunt Lottie's great silver tureen, which I admired. Also, roast goose with chestnut and sausage dressing, as well as roast beef and Yorkshire pudding, and fig cake, and mince pies, and I don't know what all. I had hazelnuts, sugared and gilded, marzipan pigs, and striped peppermint drops.

30 December

Toirc and O'Hum went to Bishop Fisher's at Salisbury to celebrate with their own family.

14 JANUARY 18~~X~~30

How strange it is to write the year. I almost had it wrong. That is why that X is there.

O'Hum and Toire are here again. Their gift to me is a buffalo-hide riding crop that I shall NOT use on Rosa, EVER.

16 JANUARY

At breakfast this morning, Mamma gave me my Christmas gifts from my Uncle King and from Uncle Billy and Aunt Adelaide.

Uncle King sent me a fan with mother-of-pearl sticks and a painted silk scene with tiny silver sequins stitched to it. His note says it is for the opera, and he hopes I will think of him.

Aunt Adelaide and Uncle Billy sent me baby house furniture, just like Feo. But they sent a music room, with a cunning little piano with real ivory keys and a gilded harp.

Lehzen was v. distressed that I could not send them my thank-you letters sooner. But I think Mamma was anxious that Captain Conroy see me open the gifts on his return after Christmas.

Madame Bourdin said to the Reverend Mr. Davys that Captain Conroy advised Mamma not to permit me to open my gifts until he was there. She heard him say it before everyone went home for Christmas. She asked if that is the same as interfering with a message from His Majesty.

Mr. Davys is of a milder temperament than Madame Bourdin. He said Mamma knows what she means to do, and she does so. "And after all . . . harrumph . . . Christmas has twelve days."

I wanted to say, Christmas has not twenty-two days, though, has it? That is how long I've had to wait.

But I have written my notes now, worded exactly as Mamma and Captain Conroy thought right. Lehzen sent the letters out.

25 JANUARY

V. cold in the rooms out of the sun. The wind is damp in the chimneys and stifles the fires. I was sitting on

Mamma's dressing table bench for Mrs. MacLeod to come and do my hair. Lehzen was in the window seat. We had sent for Lutie to put the fire to rights.

I saw there was a letter that had not burned up, which was caught on the grate, and I honestly did not know if it had been tossed there on purpose, so I took it up and glanced at it. Not meaning to read it, truly, but how could I not when I saw what it was?

It was from Aunt Adelaide. She counsels Mamma not to take so much advice from Captain Conroy, for he does not know the way things ought to be done, she says. Mamma must let me have other friends besides his family — for I might be a queen in the future!

That's all I saw, Feo, but I saw it. I dropped the letter then, and Lutie came and kindled the fire with it.

But, Feo, I wish my dear aunt would not say such a thing. It must be very painful for her to think so. I could only be queen if Aunt Adelaide has no child, and she probably will. Or if Uncle Cumberland and Georgie and my cousins all were to die first, for my Duke Papa was younger than his brothers, except Uncle Cambridge, I think. Uncle Cambridge is the Governor-General of Hanover, since my Uncle King is Elector but cannot live there and do the governing every day. My cousin George of Cambridge is the same age as Georgie Cumberland and I — I mean, I am in the middle, but we were born the same year. Even supposing I were to rise so high, it would be so far in the future, it scarcely bears thinking of <u>now</u>.

Aunt Soap says she's certain, since Uncle Cumberland was in battle, and is "off" sometimes, we owe it to patriotism to be tolerant of him. But I am glad Uncle Billy is older than Uncle Cumberland, and I am glad Aunt Adelaide is a good, young duchess, and will probably have a darling baby soon, and surely a healthy one this time. I do not like to think of Uncle Cumberland as King.

I am sleepy. There are too many things to think of these days. I said that to Uncle Leopold and he said he understood what I meant by it.

10 FEBRUARY

Shall I ever see dear de Spaeth again? It is so unbearable to think one can never be with someone for whom one has such natural affection.

Indeed, I envy her being with you, Feo.

16 FEBRUARY

Uncle Sussex's birthday. He had a literary evening, which he prefers to a party. He did end up singing Scotch songs at the piano with his children Captain Augustus and Miss d'Este. His voice is quite as splendid as the opera.

I gave him my drawing of "Cornelia and the Gracchi," which I did from an etching of an ancient Roman family. Uncle was entertained by my sending my Old Testament biblical picture, "Hagar and Ishmael," to New Zealand. He knows a fellow at the American embassy, who undertakes to get me an autograph from Fenimore Cooper, the author of *The Last of the Mohicans*. In exchange, I will send Uncle's friend my painting, "View of the Serpentine in Autumn." I am v. pleased.

I wish someone would take me to see the wild animal tamer and charmer of deadly cobras that Captain d'Este saw at Astley's Amphitheatre. It sounds v. amusing and informational. An animal trainer must be brave not to be always thinking he may be eaten at any time.

17 FEBRUARY

Mamma remarks that my Uncle King's health lately has been sinking fast. All of us children of his family line must have official guardians voted on by Parliament sometime, I take it. If a grown-up King is too ill to rule, as Grandfather George III was when he was old, there must be a guardian called a Regent to rule for him. And if the next heir is not old enough to rule, there would have to be a Regent the nation could trust.

According to all Mamma hears, it would be prudent to have my educational progress approved before poor Uncle King grows any worse. That would prove the Kensington System according to which I am being taught is a good one. O'Hum is afraid Uncle King might say Mamma has not taught me in the proper English style. He says His Majesty might take it into his head to put it in his will that Uncle Cumberland should be my guardian, or Uncle Cambridge. They would not do things O'Hum's way, as Mamma does! Mamma and O'Hum insist she is best to be my Regent. The better to guard my interests in England — that is how she explains it to me. That ought to count for something with His Majesty.

Oh, fie. I think Mamma is worrying over nothing. Who would take a child from the care of her mother? What stuff!

LATER

Now I understand. Captain Conroy thinks Mamma should have it in writing, legally binding, that she would be my Regent until I turn <u>eighteen</u> — or <u>twenty-one</u>! I think he expects Parliament will increase her income merely on account of her being named.

So Mamma is going to devise some examination I will have to endure, to prove the Kensington System is the best way to educate a modern child. I wonder whom she will have to hear me recite my lessons. She says it must be someone more important and impartial than my own instructors, if it is to impress anyone.

I fear such an examination, Feo. It will be torture to be tested, by strangers, with so much at stake.

I hate Captain Conroy. He is a terrible influence on Mamma, him with his bishop in the family. Mamma has decided my examination will be by the bishops! But of course, not Toire's great-uncle, old Bishop Fisher, who says whatever one wants to hear and makes himself so friendly and gives one cinnamon lozenges. Mamma is writing to the Bishops of London and of Lincoln, and to <u>Archbishop Howley</u> of Canterbury, inviting them to ask me questions to see if I have studied sufficiently! I am v. sorry now for how lazy and slothful I have been with studying my Latin and learning division and multiplication.

Terrible thought: What if Georgie Cumberland, that awful boy, knows his Latin better than I do? Will the bishops scold me? Is it a sin to answer incorrectly if the bishops have told one to learn something and one forgets? What if they did not tell one directly, but they think one should know it by a certain age? I listen to the sermons every Sunday in church, but one cannot remember all of it. The Bible is a v. large book. And so is the *History of Great Britain*.

The Bishop of London was with my Papa the morning I was born, and so was Archbishop Howley. Perhaps they will be kind to me for my Papa's memory's sake.

But I do not see why the Reverend Mr. Davys cannot report to them what sort of scholar I am. He knows what I have learned and what I am only now learning. He knows about the Kensington System. He knows I work at my lessons every day except the Sabbath. Even when we were on holiday, I did my studying.

Mr. Davys recommended I fortify my fainting heart by reading the Bible story about Daniel in the lion's den. I did so, and it says Habakkuk made pottage (that means bean soup, I think) and took it to Daniel. I don't see how that's supposed to make me feel better.

LATER

I have been trying to be brave about my examination. But I know I am not sufficiently brave. One thinks of courage as a virtue of the battlefield. I regret that I have already shown myself lacking in this virtue.

If I had been brave enough to speak to Captain Conroy directly, instead of sending my dear Baroness, perhaps I would have saved Mamma from being hurt and de Spaeth from being banished.

My conscience is not clear on this matter. I am a mere child, and should not have to govern the behaviour of adults. But I particularly wish not to be a coward. I am a Princess.

My Mamma is a Duchess who was born a Princess. Captain Conroy does not take orders that he does not like from either of us. Mamma gives him credit for more obedience than he provides. The plain fact is, <u>she</u> obeys <u>him</u>. And if I obey her as I ought, she makes me obey him. That does not seem right.

It is a problem for which I cannot find the key.

But I must be brave about being tested. It would be far worse if Uncle Cumberland were to be my guardian.

28 FEBRUARY

The Reverend Mr. Davys asked if I read Daniel. I said, "Yes."

He said, "And what moral has the story?"

I said, "If one wishes not to be lionized, one should eat a dish of bean pottage?"

He said he was pretty certain that was not it.

I ought to stop writing and begin to study my lesson books.

1 March

Before the bishops' questions, the Reverend Mr. Davys tells me, we had better do the Monarchs of England: Lancasters, Yorks, and Tudors. We must also discuss William and Mary and the Colonies.

I said I should like to discuss a question with the bishops that I have in mind about a bit of Scripture. As long as they are listening. (I think I ought to get <u>something</u> for all my trouble, don't you, Feo?)

Mr. Davys thought they would be charmed to be asked, but he prays me tell him what text I will cite.

Now I will have to think of a good question.

2 March

No good ideas.

3 March

Nothing I can ask.

4 MARCH

I must come up with something.

5 MARCH

Can only think of blockhead questions.

6 MARCH

Went to Lambeth Palace, where the Archbishop lives. All the bishops had gathered there. I really do not admire red brick, even when it is aged. Inside, everything is v. shining, with lots of wax on the woodwork and brass knobs and so on. One cannot help leaving smudges.

His Grace the Archbishop Howley seems to be bald. He wears an old-fashioned white wig that leaves his forehead uncovered all the way back to a place about even with the front of his ears. The effect is that his face is like a very large hard-cooked egg with a napkin laid across the top to keep it warm.

(When I reread what I have written, it sounds as if it is an amusing sight. However, it is not. Foolish though it was, I felt again my childhood horror that His Grace intended somehow to set me afire!) Yet he was not unkind to me.

The Right Reverend Bishop of London has thick, white hair of his own. He is shaped rather plump, like a hot chocolate pot, but billowy. His Grace the Bishop of Lincoln has wiry umber hair, a moderate amount of it, and piercing, small, dark eyes. He clears his throat every now and then in a most startling fashion that sounds a good deal as if he is growling. He did not smile much all afternoon. (I attempted a smile toward him, but v. quickly saw he disapproved of it.)

Mamma was wearing a dark grey cashmere coat with black fur trim and a visiting suit of heavy grey silk sultana. She looked v. beautiful, probably the most beautiful, sad lady widow they ever saw.

I was wearing a white twill merino frock with blue velvet bows and Swiss buttons. I think it is v. infantile, but no one cares for my opinion. And my long, blue pelisse (one of my favourite cloaks), and my fisher-fur muff, but, of course, I took them off once we were inside, out of the cold.

At first, I think, Their Graces were not certain how to begin. We sat down. The chairs in Archbishop Howley's study are large and hard, upholstered with dark green plush that is faded to burnt sienna on the sides facing the windows. I wished Mamma would not be there. However, she was.

They asked me baby questions. Can I say the Lord's Prayer? Do I know the name of the river that flows through London? What subjects have my Masters been teaching me?

I said, "Reading, writing, adding, subtracting, drawing, dancing, music, history, geography, Scripture reading, languages, and orthography." I might as well not have told them the whole list, because all they heard was the last word, and they tested me from the spelling list Lehzen had provided: instrument; regiment; testament; complexion; phlogiston; antediluvian; scurvy; decorum; account; beaux.

I got all of them right, because, after all, Lehzen had me study them especially. The archbishop asked me if I know what "decorum" means. They did not appear to care whether I know about flood, fire, or disease. Perhaps they think everyone knows what a regiment is and what a complexion should be.

I remarked that "beaux" is really a French word, and then they gave me some French spelling to do. London said, "*Fleurs-de-lis*," and Lincoln said, "*Aiglon*." London said, "*Verrière*," and Lincoln said, "*Vérité*." I pronounced them in French and said "lily flowers," "eaglet," "stained-glass window," "truth," and spelled them. His Grace the Archbishop said my accent is v. lovely and like Mamma's.

Then London said, "How much German do you speak?" And I remembered the Captain always forbidding us to speak German, so I said, "I read it more accurately than I speak it." Lincoln said, "If it please Your Highness, say something in German," and I couldn't think of ANYTHING clever, so I just said, "*Kein Blumenkohl, bitte schön*," and translated it, "No cauliflower, pretty please." That seemed to be enough. At least, London smiled and said, "Let us see what Your Highness knows about the world, then."

Remembering tires me. I'll write more tomorrow.

7 MARCH

On with the tale of my ordeal. We did globes for a bit, capitals, northernmost seaports, ice-free harbours, principal products, forms of government. By and by, they began to open my lesson books, history and arithmetic and also

Latin, to search for details on which to question me in the chapters Mamma told them I have mastered.

They asked a good number of Catechism questions and I recited the answers, but they did not ask what the answers meant.

They asked me to read a poem, then handed me one stanza of Mr. Keats's "Ode to a Nightingale." (I do not know if Mamma or Mr. Davys recommended it. Uncle Sussex is the one who gave it to me to see if I would like it as a recitation piece, for it was written the same week I was born. But I do not have it by memory yet.) However, I read it with good feeling.

Thou wast not born for death, immortal Bird!
No hungry generations tread thee down;
The voice I hear this passing night was heard
In ancient days by emperor and clown:
Perhaps the self-same song that found a path
Through the sad heart of Ruth, when, sick for home,
She stood in tears amid the alien corn;
The same that oft-times hath
Charm'd magic casements, opening on the foam
Of perilous seas, in faery lands forlorn.

London talks more than Lincoln. I would almost say he chatters, but that does not sound as dignified as a bishop is. He does run on. Dr. Howley is far more stately.

I began to wonder if the Reverend Mr. Davys had told them I wanted to ask a question. For I had thought of one, finally, the night before, and no one but the bishops probably could offer me assistance with it. I was not certain they would think it a good question, though.

I had told Mr. Davys the text. It is the v. end of St. Mark's Gospel. I read it one day because I am the sort of person who sometimes wants to know the end I am reading toward. I know it occasionally spoils a surprise to do so. But it doesn't spoil a holiday in Ramsgate to know one is on the way to Ramsgate, when one is thirsty and hungry and bored and having to change horses in Strood, does it?

At long last, Lincoln said, "Your good instructor, Davys, has informed us Your Highness has a curiosity about the Gospel. Would you like to air your puzzle, dear Princess?" I did not trust his calling me "dear," not one particle. He seemed impatient, and I feared he would think my question silly.

"I want to ask you, Your Graces," I said (and I wished

Mamma were not there, for she will tell Captain Conroy, and I know he will not understand), "about how Our Lord said we may test if we believe, truly."

"Go on," Dr. Howley said. He and London seemed more interested than Lincoln did.

"Well," I said (trying not to speak too quietly, for Lincoln seemed a bit deaf), "the verse says this:

These signs shall follow them that believe. In my name they shall cast out devils. They shall speak with new tongues. They shall take up serpents, and if they drink any deadly thing, it shall not hurt them. They shall lay lands on the sick, and they shall recover.

"I am just a child," I began, "and very imperfect and needing improvement. I have never cast out a devil. For a very long time, though, I did say my prayers on every occasion I went into the rose drawing room, because I was afraid of the ghost of my sister Feodora's dormouse that was in the cushion Sir John sat on. We didn't know if it would haunt the drawing room or the tiger lily bed where we buried it. And no ghost ever bothered me, so I thought perhaps that is something like casting out a devil.

"And you can see, I am learning to speak in new tongues. That is, Latin is not new, but it is new to me.

"My Mamma will tell you it is true that when we were traveling back from Ramsgate, the water at Faversham was VERY bad, and everyone got ill from it, but I did not. I cannot say why, for I certainly had to have some when I brushed my teeth, but I only rinsed and did not drink it — perhaps that's why. So I don't know if one can call that a sign.

"And then, when we got home, I laid my hands on Dash, and he recovered from being very ill. Still, he is only a dog. Perhaps that doesn't count with matters of religion.

"So, it seems to me I must go on trying to improve myself according to the Scripture. Now, I would like to be brave, like my Duke Papa and my Uncle York and Lord Nelson. I suppose that is where the serpents have to come into things.

"And here is my question: How am I ever to learn how to take up serpents, if my Mamma will not let my Uncle Sussex and Baroness Lehzen take me to Astley's Amphitheatre, This Month Only, to see the Wild Animal Tamer and Charmer of Deadly Cobras?"

Unfortunately, I received no answer. The Bishop of London had some strange sort of snorting, coughing seizure that sounded almost as if he were laughing at the same time. The Bishop of Lincoln whacked him rather severely between the shoulder blades. Archbishop Howley said he must consult with some doctors of divinity on the matter. We adjourned.

8 MARCH

I regret that I wore new slippers to Lambeth Palace. They were too stiff, and I have blisters on both heels. Toire noticed how gingerly I was walking. I said it was nothing, but v. soon afterward, Captain Conroy had Dr. Silas summoned to find out if there is some weakness in my shins or knees.

My word, anyone would think he had a wager on me for the Derby.

Feo, I have learned the truth of my position.

A few days ago (is it truly only days?) I was at my lessons with the Reverend Mr. Davys, and we worked all morning at Latin. I asked, v. politely, why we did not put it aside and take up my history book, for Latin wearies me when it's all rules and no new vocabulary.

Mr. Davys looked at Lehzen when I asked, I saw him. But I thought he was looking to her for sympathy, having in common such a lazy student. (I knew Mamma had been praised by Their Graces for how well I have progressed. As it had turned out, though, I had not had such a difficult time with their examination. I do not think they expected even so much from me. Yet I knew I could have been more perfect and complete in my answers, had I not been so nervous.)

Mr. Davys rather abruptly caught up his watch chain and remarked that it was later than he had realized, and begged to be excused to go and attend to an engagement he had with an elderly cousin.

When he had gone, Lehzen said, v. smoothly, "Your Highness, I believe Mr. Davys mentioned you were drawing up a list of the Monarchs of England. Pray, continue with that task." So I fetched my book and opened it to the page we'd been at, where there was a sort of family tree charted to show the succession of my family to the Throne of England. The list folds out sideways, and the day before, I had noted that it came only as far as Great-Grandfather George II, and that the last section seemed to have been cut off.

I am always sorry to see a book damaged, so I was pleased to see someone had found the loose page and returned it to its place and pasted it in. So I began to copy the next lines.

Every name had under it the dates of birth and death. Of course, my eye went searching for the names I love best, now that they were added to the roll of honour. All of Grandfather and Grandma'am's fifteen children were arrayed across the page. There was my Papa's name: Edward Augustus, Duke of Kent and Strathearn, Earl of Dublin, born 1767, died 1820. Not yet fifty-three years old — how tragic!

I copied it onto my chart, then went back and began on all the others. Of course, I automatically did the subtractions to see how old everyone else was — or is — and something did not seem quite right. Father was listed between Aunt Charlotte of Württemberg, whom I can't remember, and Aunt Augusta — and Aunt Augusta, his younger sister, is sixty-one years old. Of course, I realized my childish error immediately — I had never given a thought to how my Papa would have been growing older all these years. He would now be approaching sixty-three years old.

But then — it sounds so stupid and dull, telling it thus, step-by-step, but in truth, my mind was flying open v. suddenly — I saw Uncle Billy's and Uncle Cumberland's dates of birth. Uncle Billy — 1765. Uncle Cumberland — 1771. Uncle King — 1762. Uncle Cumberland is fifty-nine. Uncle Billy is sixty-five years old. And Uncle King is sixty-eight. When my Uncle King dies, just as Georgie said, Uncle Billy, the next oldest, will become King. And then — my Papa would follow. As his heir, that means —

Oh, surely, Aunt Adelaide will have a little prince soon! Or a Princess Royal!

But if she does not — I must be Queen.

I looked up at Lehzen, and she was not reading or embroidering. She was gazing at me with such compassion and tenderness, I knew she was aware of my discovery.

"I never saw this page before," I said.

"It was not thought necessary that you should," she said softly.

"I see I am closer to the Throne than I thought."

"So it is, my dear Princess."

"I shall in all probability be the cousin of a King or Queen. Aunt Adelaide's child . . ."

Then — oh, Feo, you cannot know how my heart and stomach were jumping about! Dear Lehzen shook her head, and said, "Dearest child, Her Highness the Duchess of Clarence, your good Aunt Adelaide, is not expected to have any healthy baby. She has said to me, herself, that although she hopes and prays, she is not really robust enough for it. Whatever rumors may contend."

I could not believe what I was hearing! Aunt and Uncle want a child so badly! I am sure most people would be pleased and proud to think they might one day rise to the Throne, and own so much responsibility to the nation. And so I am, Feo. But at what cost to happiness! It seemed to my confused heart that Lehzen was almost cruel to go on and say it:

"In all probability, you will be Queen of England."

No crown will ever weigh on me more heavily than

those words! What I replied was not a boast, Feo, truly, but more of a Solemn Oath.

"I will be good at it," I said. Or, to be more precise, that was what I meant to say. Lehzen saw what a state I was in, and she came over quickly and embraced me, and she only heard me say, "I will be good." I'm afraid my thought was more practical than virtuous! Yet it pleased her so well, she has since then mentioned it to several people, and under the circumstances, I cannot very well correct her!

Oh, Feo, have you always known? Truly, I did not see it! Toire called me a "sly boots" because she thought I must certainly have realized my position all along. I finally convinced her that I had not, and now she behaves as if, mentally, I am sadly deficient, not to have thought of it!

Indeed, my feelings are drawn so violently in so many directions, I hardly know that she is not correct!

LATER

Toire almost caught me with my journal open in my lap. Not only can she be quiet noisily, she can also knock on a door so it sounds like a mouse in the wall, and then when she comes in on one, she says, "No one answered, so I entered." She hears a lot of conversation this way. For <u>her</u> to call <u>me</u> "sly boots" is to mistake me for her own equal.

Fortunately, Dash had just taken up Lehzen's muff and was trying to shake it to bits, and Fanny was v. distressed at Dashy's bad behaviour, for she has known better for years. So I had tucked my book under my seat cushion in order to rescue the muff.

Toire has started calling me "Your Royal Highness," and I think that is an impertinence, for I do not know that I am entitled yet to be so addressed. Besides, I heard her say to Mr. Coutts that she is my "most intimate friend." And to Dr. Silas, that she fears I suffer from nervous frailty and must be overseen continuously for my own good.

All, not true. I asked her to go away. She went.

Everyone acts as though it is a great relief to <u>them</u> not to have to conceal "my station" from me any longer. Mamma said, "Now you will understand why we must be ever vigilant to protect you." Captain Conroy said, "Now you know why Cumberland would just as soon you were to disappear."

I said to him, " 'England expects that every man will do his duty,' as Lord Nelson said. I am sure my Uncle

Cumberland knows, beyond all things, what his duty is, and to whom he owes it."

The Captain said that my tender years prevent him from telling me all he might about Certain Information he receives from Certain Sources. He said he is confident, as I mature, I will better appreciate how necessary his management is to my Destiny.

I did not reply, but only gave him a stony look. I would have liked to ask him to go away. If he were not her father, I might even be able to like Toire. Although, I think not.

I do not understand why no one seems to realize, I will not be Queen before my poor old Uncle King and my dear, jolly Uncle Billy are gone. I do not like to think of my sweetest Aunt Adelaide suffering such sadness, never to have a child of her own, and to be widowed. I TRULY do not like to think of what happened to Aunt Princess Charlotte. Uncle Leopold is still grieving for her, that is plain.

I do look forward to discussing this turn of events with Uncle Leopold and Stocky. Every night when I say my prayers, I ask that Uncle will not go off to Greece. I could not bear it.

4 April
Carling Sunday

Only a week until Easter. The primroses have come into bloom, also the hyacinths near the round pond. Lady Northumberland told me, if one finds a pea pod with nine peas in it, one can put it over one's door lintel on Carling Sunday (as they call Palm Sunday in the North Country and Scotland), and the next man who comes in will be the man one will marry. I asked Cook for some new peas to shell, and after I'd opened about four dozen of them, I found one with nine peas. I brought it upstairs directly, and put it over the door. However, Feo, the only one who came in was Mrs. MacLeod with yesterday's late post, which was a letter for Mamma from Coburg, from our Uncle Prince Ernest. It is too bad I could not leave the peas longer, but as soon as Lady Northumberland left, Mamma told Lehzen she wouldn't have me carrying on in such a vulgar fashion, and I had to send the peas back to Cook.

However, the letter included two v. handsome ivory miniatures of our cousins, Albert and Ernest. The artist was v. good, and they are v. handsome boys. I should like to be able to paint as well.

16 April

Weather is HOT for this time of year.

It has occurred to me that, should I become Queen, I will be able to order Captain Conroy to go to India. I hate the way he speaks to Mamma. She does not think it insolence, but I do.

I should like to cast him out.

26 May

My eleventh birthday two days ago was <u>VERY</u> happy. Uncle Leopold came, and he told me he has decided <u>not</u> to be King of Greece! What wonderful news! He says they will have trouble with Turkey, and his affectionate connexions with England would complicate matters for everyone.

Feo, you will never guess what he brought me as my present. It is a big silver tureen, like Aunt Princess Lottie's. And you will never guess how he got it. He drizzled a good deal of gold floss, and used that to pay for it! I imagined a great heap of golden threads, but he said gold is worth so much, one can turn a little of it into quite a bit more silver.

He said the golden floss was only a ball as big as his fist. The tureen is so big, I could wash Dashy in it.

Perhaps I shall. It is <u>my</u> tureen.

And, Feo, you'll never guess where I've been! Before dinner, Uncle Sussex and Lord Paget and Lehzen took me to the circus at Astley's! We saw Bengal Tigers and Lions of the Savannah! Also, ladies in frilly, spangled dresses riding backward and standing up on white horses with plumes of purple and red ostrich feathers. It was VERY jolly. Uncle Sussex said Mr. William Blake's poem to the Tiger when we walked past its cage. The Tiger thrashed its tail and bared its fangs, but then it did not roar, it only yawned. Still, it was shocking to see such terrible teeth.

No deadly cobras, though. Lord Paget said, "Well, then, that's something pleasant to look forward to." I was very, VERY amused.

LATER

Mamma lent me a page from her letter from Grandmamma. I copy it here:

"My blessings and good wishes for the day which gave you the sweet blossom of May! May God preserve and protect the valuable life of that lovely flower from all the dangers that will beset her mind and heart! The rays of the sun are scorching at the height to which she may one day attain. It is only by the blessing of God that all the fine qualities He has put into that young soul can be kept pure and untarnished."

I am sure, Feo, that all grandmothers harbour such feelings. But I think our own dear Grandmamma says it v. touchingly. She is a v. old lady, yet her writing is remarkably stylish.

Lo, even back so far in the ledger — MORE COW HISTORY:

Butterfat — Lbs. per Annum

Rose	*929*	*Melchett*	*414*
Diamond	*925*	*Livia*	*603*
Winner	*968*	*Lily*	*816*
Irene	*977*	*Molly*	*860*
Agnes	*642*	*Polly*	*780*
Nancy	*771*	*Dolly*	*900*
Vinia	*550*		

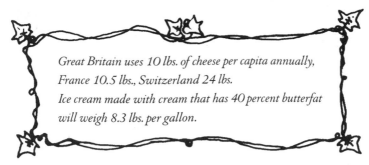

*Great Britain uses 10 lbs. of cheese per capita annually,
France 10.5 lbs., Switzerland 24 lbs.
Ice cream made with cream that has 40 percent butterfat
will weigh 8.3 lbs. per gallon.*

Whoever wrote this drew charmingly — this is a v. good ivy vine around the cheese and ice cream.

26 JUNE

Oh, Feo. Two days ago my Uncle the King passed on to Divine Justice and Reward. I thought I could never again feel so bereft as I did when Uncle York died. Now I think, the older one is, the sharper the pain. One does not become used to it, because each time it is worse. More is lost.

If there is wisdom to comfort one, I wish it would speak to me.

A messenger came full speed from Wellington at Windsor to my Uncle Sussex and Aunt Soap.

Uncle William IV rules England.

Uncle Sussex said, "So the earth spins." Then he went aside and wept.

Aunt Soap had hysterics and needed smelling salts. Since de Spaeth is no longer here, no one knew at first where to find them.

As I write, I am clutching my little brooch of my Uncle King's dear face, which I shall see no more. I am weeping, too.

27 JUNE

Captain Conroy became impatient with Mamma. She said it would be shocking to write the Chief Mourner, Uncle William, about business — about increasing my income based on my being Heiress Presumptive — and Uncle King George IV just now dead. Captain Conroy thumped his fist on the shiny black Chinese writing desk, and declared she must be the first to advance a suggestion, for no one in high places would ever seek her thoughts based on their regard for them or her. But the government will surely send a recommendation to Parliament now about who is to be my Regent.

He has no understanding of Mamma's natural delicacy and Royal courtesy and taste. Uncle Leopold has said it:

Too often, the effect is that the Captain seems determined to blunt her refined sensibilities.

Even I can see it will make Uncle Billy want to knock the Captain down with a boat hook. Why don't Mamma and the Captain see it?

At least they have to send any messages to Uncle Billy through the good old Duke of Wellington, because he's Prime Minister. Perhaps he will talk them out of it.

Aunt Adelaide sent me a brief note — alas, on paper bordered in black. She wished to assure me, during these sad days, of Uncle Billy's and her great affection for me. Her words are a comfort. Frail straws on the tide. The world has changed overnight. It does not seem to be the same world.

17 JULY

Uncle King George's State Funeral was two days ago — I am exhausted. Black and purple everywhere, mostly black crape by the yard, draped on everything and everyone. The scent of flowers and swags of cypress was too heavy and sweet in the heat. Uncle Billy wore a long, dark purple

velvet cape. Georgie Cumberland carried the train of it —
I believe that was Aunt Adelaide's idea.

Uncle Billy said later, "My dear brother is no longer
suffering the indignity of mortality."

I said, "Uncle, is that how one bears up under missing
the dead whom we love?"

He put his hand on mine, just a little tap because of
his gout. "Ah, well, Little Vic, by my age you don't expect
to be apart from them for so long." He said it v. cheerfully,
though.

A solemn thought occurred to me. It seemed to me for
a moment that he and I might, after all, be the only ones
there to share a fate others only imagine.

"Uncle," I said, "will you like being King, do you
think?"

"Oh, well, as to that," he said, quoting Admiral Nelson
as he often does, "England expects that every man will do
his duty." And, although he was wearing that immense
purple train and all about us was so sad, he winked
at me.

"I suppose England expects it of every girl, as well," I
said.

"Of every hand on board, Little Vic," he said.

19 July

Oh, fie on the Kensington System! How entirely dreadful! Mamma and the Captain have now decided that <u>once or twice a year</u> they should like me to have examinations by the Archbishop and London and Lincoln <u>and</u> by the Lord President of His Majesty's Privy Council <u>and</u> the Lord Chief Justice of the King's Bench! I shall be on trial like a common criminal!

20 July

The Reverend Mr. Davys tells me that in India, among the Dravidians, a v. old society, it is still believed that ancestors may be reborn as calves in order to nourish the people with their milk. For this reason, cows are treated with a degree of respect and are not eaten.

A little knowledge is a dangerous thing. I felt odd about the sauerbraten and noodles at luncheon. But I am persuaded, even were that not an heathen superstition, it could not have been a Dravidian cow that we were eating.

26 July

Today I participated in the investiture of King Wilhelm I of Württemberg, as a Knight of the Garter. It is a great honour for Uncle Billy to make King Wilhelm a K.G., and for me to be included in the event.

This is particularly so, since Uncle Billy says he does not like "all that fuss." He does not even want to have a big celebration for his own coronation — he says it's a waste of money and a waste of a good day. I certainly hope he is joking! I rather enjoyed today's ceremonies.

I wore my mourning gown, which is black silk tabby, and a LONG veil of black chambray, and I stood to the left of Uncle Billy's throne. I felt v. grown up, not wearing white.

27 July

Mr. Grant, the Member of Parliament from Inverness (and some other towns) in Scotland, stood up in the House of Commons to suggest that they ask Uncle Billy who should be my Regent, should anything happen to him.

Mr. Grant said, pretty directly, "No one prefers it should be a foreign king."

Lehzen is the one who told me this. She explained that Hanover, in Germany, for many years has been connected to the English throne. But the law of Hanover permits no female rulers, so I am now the Presumptive Heiress of England, but Uncle Cumberland is Presumptive Heir of Hanover. If I were to become Queen, <u>he</u> would be <u>my</u> next-in-line, until I married and had Issue. (That means a baby.) So, no one really thinks he would be the best one to watch after my interests.

I wonder if anyone thinks Mamma can protect my interests and England's interests against Captain Conroy's interests. I wonder if they think of it at all.

28 JULY

Oh, dear, no time for writing.

Breakfasted at Palace of St. James with the Württembergers. It became v. awkward, however. In fact, dreadful. I did not understand why, at first. I am not entirely sure I do, even now.

I was sitting with Aunt Adelaide and some others, who were speaking fondly of Lake Constance. Uncle Billy was rather bouncing around the morning room, talking to EVERYONE — he seemed to be enjoying himself immensely, I must say.

He had just come over near us when a rather tall fellow opened the glass doors at the side of the room and came in. He is someone I know I've seen before — I have the impression he is in the Navy — but to whom I had never happened to be introduced. He seemed startled when he came in, as though he didn't know who was here, but he came over directly and said good morning to Aunt and Uncle.

"Little Vic," Uncle said, "this is your cousin Adolphus FitzClarence. What d'ye want, Addy?"

Mamma was nearby, and I saw out of the corner of my eye that she had suddenly gone all bristles and fire-irons.

Mr. FitzClarence said, "Willie Paget, Governor — thought we'd have a spot of sculling later. Sorry to barge in on you when you're running before the wind — didn't know it was Official in here." Then, to me, he said, "Your Servant, Your Highness," and he bowed v. prettily, but without a trace of a smile, and walked off across the room.

Mamma, meanwhile, had snapped her fan shut, and bunched her skirt around her and had stood up, all at once, and in four steps she was beside my chair. And she was furious, I could tell.

"The carriage is sent for," she announced to me. Then she turned to Aunt Adelaide — NOT to His Majesty Uncle Billy — and said, "I shall take Victoria home now."

Uncle Billy said, "Nonsense, nonsense, we all need to take our ease after all the falderal." He held up a "weather finger," as he says, to a servant with a tray of Italian coffee cups. Aunt Adelaide was appearing v. distressed. I stood there, quite dumb, thinking of remarks Georgie Cumberland has made.

"I am afraid," Mamma said icily, "a name has been mentioned that I cannot condone in this innocent child's presence."

"My own name, by God!" Uncle Billy said to her — and his voice was soft, dangerously soft, I might say, like the sea before a storm. "My name, and my good son wearing it."

"Certainly not suitable in the presence of the Heiress Presumptive!" Mamma said. I believe I may say, she fairly hissed.

"'Suitable' anywhere I am King, Madam! Under my own roof, Madam! I believe I am lately King of all the roofs and names hereabouts, and all the Heirs and Presumptions, as well, by God!"

Aunt Adelaide was wringing her handkerchief into string, but Mamma made me stand and curtsy and leave. I felt I should die of humiliation.

LATER

It is so difficult to write these days. Mamma has been sleeping ill, and even late at night, I must be wary of her pacing around.

Walking with Lehzen this afternoon, I had the explanation for Mamma's actions at Uncle Billy's. I realized I had heard most of it before, whether or not I recognized its meaning at the time. Uncle Billy is not as simple a soul as he seems to be.

Lehzen says, long, long ago, he had another lady, who

was a beautiful actress, Mrs. Dorothy Jordan. He had not met Aunt Adelaide yet — indeed, she had not even been born yet! Grandfather George III would not permit him to marry when he came home from the sea. Their domestic arrangements were not proper, and Uncle has quite a few <u>natural</u> sons and daughters! The one I met is a younger son. They are all grown up now. (Indeed, one grew up and went to India and died there, before my Papa met Mamma.) Mrs. Jordan died before Uncle met his dear Queen Adelaide.

Because he was the Duke of Clarence, and his children are not accepted as relatives, their name is FitzClarence. Mamma is v. correct that they are not to be received in the best society. To treat them as if they were acceptable would seem to approve publicly of Uncle's sins.

Yet Aunt Adelaide is so good, she loves them for Uncle's sake, and Lehzen says they are quite at home all together. I must say, I received a good impression of Mr. FitzClarence. His voice is rich, quiet, thrilling, and manly. Lehzen says Mrs. Jordan was famous for her enchanting voice.

The world is a v. surprising place, some days.

2 August

I yearn for Ramsgate. Feo, I yearn for your kindness. How is the dear Baroness de Spaeth? I know she must miss me dreadfully, for so I miss her. I miss Uncle King. I miss Uncle York. I miss Brocky. I miss my Duke Papa, though I never knew him. I am a v. sad girl.

8 August

Captain Conroy and Mamma have decided we shall not go directly to Ramsgate for our holidays. They want to introduce me to more people — my people, they say, as if I were already Queen. I don't know which will make me more uncomfortable — riding in the carriage over hill and dale, or having them show me off as if I were a dancing bear.

23 September

How long it has been since I wrote here! How great has been my anxiety, all these weeks, that my dear, precious diary would be gone when I returned! I had secreted it in the mahagony tea table in the yellow salon, and the Captain was looming over me the whole time we were preparing to leave, so I could not get it. I must say, it has been a trial not to have it. I believe I understand a bit better, now, how those steam engines work, for, all this time, I have felt like a boiler with no pressure valve.

I am glad to learn no one comes around to polish the silver tea services when we are not at home. It would be wasted work, anyway.

Now that I have my book, I still cannot even begin to tell all about our travels. Before we went to Ramsgate, we went to Malvern and stayed at Eastnor Castle — a v. curious place. It is a new castle made like an old one. It was done by Mr. Smirke, who designed the front of the British Museum — Eastnor is v. good, but rather like an immense baby house, I thought.

There are many theatrical presentations hereabouts, for it is along the Pilgrimage Route, if I may call it that, to Shakespeare's Stratford. We saw a number of plays and also heard a good deal of v. excellent music. I have written about it all in my copy book that Mamma and Lehzen read, so I shall not describe it all here. Malvern is a v. beautiful place to visit, I must say.

Thence, we went to Portsmouth, and went aboard the *Emerald* to sail to Ramsgate. The *Emerald* is the boat that brings supplies for the Royal yacht, the *Royal George*. Everywhere one goes, it is recognized and saluted — it is great fun to hear the blank shots being fired across the water. O'Hum, unfortunately (for him), is not a good sailor, and was v. much preoccupied while we were at sea.

Lady Catherine Jenkinson came with us — she is fast becoming a v. dear friend to both Lehzen and me. Her father is Lord Liverpool, and he is one of the kindest, wisest persons it is my pleasure to know. And Catherine is v. lovely, too. She was v. pleased when I told her my doll Katherine is my favourite doll.

I believe Mamma selected Lady Catherine to be one of her ladies to try to make up to us for our losing dear de Spaeth. As to that, I am with good Dr. Stockmar, who says, "Forgive much. Forget nothing."

Stocky was not with us our whole time at Ramsgate this year, for he chose to visit Coburg, Hohenlohe, Leiningen, Göttingen, and Bonn. He saw all our dearest ones, including (after you, Feo, and de Spaeth) Charles, Uncle Ernest and Grandmamma, and Cousins Ernest and Albert, and he brought us back affectionate messages from all.

He also brought Lehzen back some books in German —
one of them, by Herr von Schlegel, is about the language
and religion of India. Lehzen translates bits of it to discuss
with the Reverend Mr. Davys and Uncle Sussex. I am v. interested in India.

But the best, the merriest times we had at Ramsgate
were with Uncle Leopold. We played a great deal of chess.
I won three games against Mr. Montefiore, and two against
Uncle. (I lost many more, for we played almost every day.
Uncle says anything is better than bell and hammer!)
Each of them counsels me while I play the other, but they
only point out moves. I am the one who decides which
moves to employ.

LATER

Lehzen reminded me that I had not cleansed my teeth after supper. Now they are like pearls.

There are two topiary lions now at East Cliff: one
standing up and one lying down. You will think I have become very grown up, Feo, when I tell you that, after all
these years, I have decided I do like the sundial garden

that is overrun with woolly thyme and artemisia and white climbing roses — the one you and I used to call "the Ghost Garden." Mr. Montefiore calls it "the Garden in the Clouds." Do you remember how mysterious it is on a misty morning? He says it is even more fragrant at night than during daylight.

10 OCTOBER

Ramsgate has faded into a dream. It is plain old Kensington again, and kidney pie and sago pudding and watery vegetable marrows and apple tarts without enough cinnamon. I will be v. glad when Cook's daughter-in-law has her baby and gets done with her lying-in and Cook can come back here where she is wanted quite as much, I am sure.

17 OCTOBER

Lehzen and Lady Catherine and I dressed dolls together today. We did Shakespeare — *Twelfth Night*, though it's not Christmas. Lehzen did Countess Olivia, and Lady Catherine did Orsino, Duke of Illyria, and I did Viola.

Lady Catherine is v. musical. She is a delight. She plays the piano, and Mamma and I sing duets. It is the best way to spend time with Mamma, for she does not use so much time telling us what Captain Conroy advises-us-in-the-strongest-possible-terms — which is to say, the only way he ever advises us.

V. important confidential conversation with Uncle Leopold at Ramsgate concerning a Certain Matter. He says he can do nothing if Mamma will not preserve herself. He says I should never put myself at risk, but must get the nearest adult. No matter what happened to de Spaeth, no matter that Mamma tells me it is none of my affair.

Uncle says of course it is. Conroy is a devil, and she is my Mamma, and I dare not pretend all is as it should be, no matter how they press me to give him more power over me, over us all, and to hold my tongue. I must find the courage to hold out against his browbeating.

20 OCTOBER

Dashy is learning to bring things to me. Lady Catherine gives him my bedroom slipper and says to him, "Dispatches, Dash!" He then takes the proferred article v. delicately in his teeth, and trots to me directly. Usually, he lets me take it from him.

Since he is such an excellent messenger, I have made him a page's livery, a red-and-blue jacket and trousers. Everyone teases me about playing seamstress to my dog, and, I must confess, Dashy's not keen on his uniform. But it is v. becoming. If v. fashionable young men are called "puppies," I think it is only right to allow Dash to dress *au courant*, in the latest style. He is v. amusing.

Fanny just gazes at him from her cushion near the hearth. She is a doting auntie, but has grown rather stout of late. I think she finishes Dash's portion, and he lets her.

20 NOVEMBER

Everyone is annoyed with Uncle Billy. There has not been sufficient Reform. Not enough Englishmen can vote. Or there has been an irresponsible amount of Reform. People are voting who have no business doing so. Uncle Sussex says that when Uncle King George was ill, he did nothing for weeks, and Uncle Billy has had 48,000 documents to sign since he became King. Aunt Adelaide sits by him and bathes his cramped hand in warm water.

I do not wonder he has not written to me lately.

1 DECEMBER

When I think how I used to be able to write so often, I am quite amazed. It is not only that Lady Catherine, and my new, English governess, Lady Northumberland (who is tutoring me in Court etiquette), are about me so much of the time. It is also because my lessons take so much longer these days. If I am imperfect in my recitation, I know they all think sooner or later I shall be responsible for toppling the Throne. Yet I do not think learning Cicero has much to do with provisioning the Navy or keeping track of the East India Company.

Lord Lyndhurst, the Chancellor, stood up in the House of Lords, and called me my Mamma's "illustrious offspring." He said Mamma has done her duty by my education, and it gives everyone the best grounds to hope most favourably of my future conduct.

Anyway, Feo, you and Charles are every bit as illustrious. The House of Lords voted to name Mamma my Regent. I would be happier at this outcome if O'Hum had not immediately sat down to make a list of things the King can and cannot tell me to do. I should like to make a list of things Captain Conroy may not tell me to do. Or, that he cannot tell Mamma to tell me to do.

2 DECEMBER

Oh, Feo. I have been so blind — blinder than Lord Nelson or Uncle Cumberland, for they each lost only a single eye. But I have been totally unseeing!

Of course, Uncle Leopold will go away. He has received another invitation to be a King in another land. This time it is Belgium. I can tell that this time he will go. I see that he must. He must get over Aunt Princess Lottie's death, and accomplish more in his career. He is a v. useful statesman, and he should have the running of things. (Stocky and Lehzen both assure me this is so.)

When I think of it, it is very strange that Royal persons are the ones who must switch their loyalties and their patriotism from one country to another. In the end, it is almost as if one's family is all one has, for certain. I should not like to learn I was to be married to someone in Russia or Portugal or Denmark, and then have to turn myself into a Russian or a Portuguese or a Dane.

I am utterly miserable. The older I grow, the more I learn, the more there is that is intolerable, but that I must nonetheless bear.

Mamma and the Captain expect to receive news that the government will raise our income. They are quite jubilant these days. I fear my own Christmas will be more grievous than merry.

27 December

Oh, fie on all these grown-up children! My Christmas season is being mashed into a great mess! Uncle Billy has played a great trick on Mamma, I suppose he feels. He has told her I must change my NAME, to something ENGLISH!

Well, my name is like my Mamma's. He is still in an ill temper over Mamma objecting to his introducing my cousin FitzClarence by name, so he's giving her a taste of the same treatment. . . . But it is MY name they are juggling! And I don't believe he means simply that I should have an English girl's name. I see what he is up to, even if no one else does. If my <u>own</u> name were translated from Latin into English, it would be <u>Victory</u>! He could pretend I am named for his friend, Lord Nelson's, ship!

Uncle Billy told Mamma if I change my name to an English one, he will raise her income now, as well as going all the way back to when my Papa died! What a great lot of money that must be! I am ashamed to say, Mamma seems to think it would be worthwhile to give in. We will have no more debts.

Captain Conroy will have no more reason to become angry.

3 January 1831

Mamma does not understand the point of Uncle Billy's gambit. She has agreed to change my name by dropping

Alexandrina and adding Charlotte, because that would be more English. I do not like to think she is doing it for the money. But Certain Persons do rate such arrangements v. highly.

5 JANUARY

The newspapers have reported this matter, and it is by no means true that everyone wishes me to change my name. Some say it is impossible, for I was Christened, and that is a Sacrament and can't be changed. Others say "Charlotte" may not be fortunate, and I should be another "Elizabeth."

I am sure it would pain Uncle Leopold for me to turn into a Charlotte. I am sure it would hurt Aunt Adelaide to call me Elizabeth, for that was her baby's name who died. I might ask to be Katherine. Or Joan, like Fair Joan of Kent.

6 JANUARY

It vexes me. I am Victoria. I can see that I must be brave and give up a good deal that I love because the fate of nations requires me not to be selfish. But an Heiress Presumptive should be able to cling to her own name, at least. It is a small vessel in a great sea. But it is who I am.

I must persuade Uncle Billy to give up the joke. Mamma and the Captain simply go over the list to think of things they can arrange to do that His Majesty's objections cannot prevent. Or so it seems.

26 JANUARY

I never recorded my lovely Christmas presents. Now it strikes me as tiresome. What is the point of writing, writing, writing? I am the only one who reads these pages. If only I could see by reading them that I have gained some small increase of wisdom through all these months of misery! I <u>do</u> wish something pleasant would happen!

13 FEBRUARY

Finally, something quite lovely to look forward to. An invitation has arrived — we are to attend a drawing room at St. James, for Aunt Adelaide's birthday. Compton is making me a new frock, of satin (white — no surprise) and blond lace.

It will be a change from sitting about <u>this</u> dull palace, playing hunt the thimble with Lehzen while Mamma and O'Hum drink tea with Lord Durham and Lord Dover and exchange slighting remarks about our gracious Sovereign.

Uncle Billy is so busy, I still have had no occasion to speak to him about changing my name. This Must Stop!

26 FEBRUARY

I can't get it out of my head, Georgie Cumberland saying, "Things always seem to go from Baden to Worcester." But it is not humorous.

My dress was not right. It made me look like a big dollop of mashed potatoes. I wore my pearl necklace, but no one remarked on it.

Uncle Billy appears to be v. fatigued. He gave me a great, hearty hug, as if I were a tiny child, and it made me v. happy for a bit, and I wanted to forget my trouble. Later, though, he said to me, "Shall we get you another of these pink things, Little Vic?" (He meant an iced biscuit.) No one was in a position to overhear us just then, so I saw my chance.

"As you are so fond of me, Your Majesty, why would you have me translate my name to English?"

He said, "By God, not you, too!" and <u>laughed</u> at me! I was v. put out. I know I should have been more respectful, but my pride was hurt.

"I <u>know</u> you think it better to be named for a <u>parent</u> than for a <u>boat</u>," I said, then went on. "I quite <u>liked</u> my cousin Adolphus, Uncle," I said v. firmly. "But I notice you did not name him for <u>your</u> ship, the *Pegasus*."

Uncle Billy looked v. startled, and also rather embarrassed. I was shocked at myself for speaking to him so, but I could not take it back.

Aunt Soap happened to come up to us then, to remind me to give Aunt Adelaide the present I had brought. It was a quilted silk jewelry pouch I made for her, and embroidered with my drizzled silver thread. (I expect she has more jewels to take care of, now that she is Queen.) She was v. charmed with my handiwork, and thanked me three times.

Uncle never answered my rude remark, though he gave me quite a big embrace when we left. I did not enjoy it as much, though, for another Scene had just occurred. Lord Durham had caused some ado by insulting the Countess of Jersey, and Mamma was heard to take his part. It is too bad. The Countess's son was quite pleasant at the ball. (How long ago that seems now!)

It does not seem well-bred to discuss whether others behave in a well-bred manner. Lehzen agrees with me on this point. Feo, what would you tell me, were you here by your poor little sister's side?

9 April

There. I have torn out all the pages I wrote that were sad and angry. It is better to work at being good myself, than to complain of how I feel injustice and unkindness all around me. I will try to be happier than I have been. When I am not happy, I will try at least to be faithful and patient.

10 April

Ah, how I love the theatre! The delight of the costumes, the brilliant lights, the very, VERY FUNNY performances! How I wish Covent Garden could be part of every week! We saw *The Sleeping Beauty*. It was quite astonishing to see the thicket of briar roses grow right up out of the stage to surround poor Beauty until her Prince Charming can come to claim her. The stage set reminded me of Eastnor, that artistic little castle we visited last year near Malvern.

Later

Toire coaxed me to paint her as Beauty. She likes to array herself on the fainting couch in an attitude of "hopeful repose." She did not like my picture, though, for my brush was rather too liberal when I did the wound on her finger, and it looks as though she is holding an apple. Lady Catherine suggested we call it "Snow White," instead. I thought perhaps I could dress Dash up to be a dwarf. But Toire took offense. However, she took it for granted she could keep the painting.

16 April

Finally, I have heard La Malibran sing! *Brava, bravissima!*
Il Barbiere di Siviglia, The Barber of Seville — we attended
last week, Feo. What a stunning performance! Such a mar-
velous opera! I am uplifted beyond anything I could have
expected. <u>This</u> is what Great Art can do for one's spirit!

I carried my fan that Uncle King George gave me, and
thought fondly and sadly of him.

Uncle Billy was there, in his Lord High Admiral uniform, with its masses of undrizzled golden lace and big
cock-and-pinch hat. He sat down in the box, put his feet
up on a footstool provided for the purpose, set his hat over
his toes, and, I believe, dozed off. He spoke to no one at any
rate, and showed no interest after the overture. I think he
is v. tired from all the work a King must do. I am heartily
sorry I was unkind to him. After all, one girl's name is
nothing, compared with the rest of the world. Which, as
he says, is always right off the port bow, firing warning
shots.

24 April

After all the fuss — would you not know it, Feo? Mamma has decided she will not allow her name to be bought away from me. The Whig party is becoming more powerful now than the Tories, and she expects we shall be voted such an increase in our funds that she need not condescend to it.

I expect Uncle Billy is tired of this squabble. I hope so.

25 May

Early strawberries. Late tulips. Too much Latin. Not enough dancing.

11 June

No, No, NO! As Uncle Leopold's departure approaches, I find myself almost frantic. It is just like a nightmare here, for everyone behaves as if everything is NORMAL. What shall I do? It is the most unfortunate thing not to have a father. But I do not remember my Papa, anyway. Uncle

Leopold has been to me what a father ought to be — and now I must lose him! Am I always to be bereft?

At least Uncle Billy has finally agreed to a Coronation Ceremony. It is to be in September. Uncle Cumberland says it matters little that the last one cost 400,000 pounds. Uncle Billy says he doesn't want the falderal, his won't cost a tenth as much, and he'll be tarred before he'll let the bishops kiss him.

(I heard this from Lord Paget.)

8 AUGUST

This journal will not hold together if I keep tearing out pages and burning them. But I have been so overtired, with all my cares and studies, with never enough time to compose myself. There are always more guests to see, and they are hardly ever young people.

We shall soon leave for our holiday at Ramsgate, and I shall have more time to write there, perhaps. It will be difficult to hold to my resolve against sadness, however. It will be our last visit with Uncle Leopold for a very long time.

8 September
East Cowes, Isle of Wight

It is v. strange once more to have my treasure, my diary. I thought it gone forever. When we left Kensington for our last holiday with Uncle Leopold, I entrusted it to Lehzen, for she alone could pack it privately. But the portmanteau suitcase it was packed in went astray before we reached Ramsgate. We were all v. surprised when it arrived here at Norris Castle yesterday, all these weeks later, on the packet with the mail and newspapers.

So I take it up again, to record my days. There is much to love and admire in the world, but much that I fear I shall never understand. There is much that causes regret and sorrow.

Now I sit beside the sea on this beautiful Isle of Wight. Dear Lehzen is sitting near me, and Mamma and Sir John Conroy are farther up the strand, where the palm trees grow. It is so unusual that they flourish on English soil — I should like to paint them. Only not just now.

As I write, my Uncle William IV is most likely in his golden carriage on his way to Westminster Abbey to receive the Crown of St. Edward the Confessor.

Unless dear Aunt Adelaide has a child, I shall be the

next to wear that Crown. I should be at London with Uncle Billy for this solemn day. Even with all his cares and duties of office, I am sure he feels this in his heart as plainly as I do.

Yet, here I sit, as the sun goes in and out behind the clouds and the seabirds caw. They sound so lonely, up there so high.

I cannot write more, for my tears will melt the words.

Besides, here come Mamma and Sir John.

14 SEPTEMBER

It is not my good Uncle's fault I was not at his Coronation.

Uncle Billy is a good King, and tries to see both sides. He thought it would be best to honour the old first, and then the new — meaning me. I know that is what he wanted.

I have known for some time now that the People are actually v. fond of me. The day I was with Aunt Adelaide when Uncle went to open Parliament, she set me up on the garden wall to watch the procession pass by. And those who had been cheering, "The Queen! The Queen!" began to cry out, "Hurrah for BOTH Queens!" In that moment,

I was very, VERY joyous that I am English, and that I shall never have to leave Britain and live elsewhere.

They do not cheer my Uncle Cumberland, though — usually they call rude names. So it would have been v. improper for me to be directly behind His Majesty in the procession, so that we'd have cheers, and then have my other uncles behind us, so the cheers would stop or turn mean. I understand this. And Uncle Sussex does not deserve that, and he would be with Uncle Cumberland.

But when Sir John and Mamma learned where I was to be in the line, they chose to be insulted over MY precedence being slighted.

Parliament has already granted me a HUGE increase in my income — I will now receive 16,000 pounds of my own each year. (One of the newspapers made a joke about it. A new Bishop of Derby must be named soon, and he will get only 11,000 pounds. They said rather than Heiress Presumptive, it would have been less expensive to make me the Bishop of Derby!)

Since we are finally well set, though, Mamma and the Captain decided to get even with Uncle Billy by not letting me attend the Coronation. I still can hardly credit the cruelty and impertinence of this.

I asked Lehzen to post my letter to Uncle Billy, so he will not think it my doing. Really, I hope he knows that already. I love him and Aunt Adelaide with all my heart. It saddens me greatly, to be kept away from them.

Uncle Leopold, too — across the sea in Belgium, so very, very far away. If it were not for my beloved Lehzen, I should be entirely alone with my sadness. No one else understands.

LATER

Now I've written that, I see it is not quite true. I am blessed to have as many people about me as I do, who love me and <u>try</u> to understand.

I was moaning and complaining to the Reverend Mr. Davys about how fearful I am of all the demands placed upon me by — well, I never like to say to him by whom. He knows Certain Persons are harder than others.

Moreover, I said, "What can I do, when those I love keep leaving?"

He said then, "Your Royal Highness, shall I recommend the closure of the Gospel of Matthew? Our Lord said, 'Lo, I am with you always, even unto the end of the world.'"

Well, Belgium is, at least, not the end of the earth. I shall remind myself of that.

My last evening together with Uncle Leopold I was weeping, and he took my hand in both of his and held it to his heart.

"I will tell you, now, something I have never revealed to you before," he said. "It is something Count Esterhazy told me long ago, that I have kept to myself all this time, lest the mystery and power of it should be dispelled. Perhaps your mamma knows, I cannot say.

"Esterhazy told me that it has long been common knowledge among the Gypsies in Hungary that there was a Gypsy at Gibraltar when your Father was there, who read his fortune for him. She told him three things.

"First — that he would never be King. Second — that he would attain supreme happiness, and would die soon thereafter."

I sobbed when he said that, but I managed to say, "I am glad he was happy."

"The third prediction was the most important," Uncle then said gently. "The Gypsy told your Papa he would have a daughter who would be a very great Queen, of a very great nation.

"And, you see — the good woman will turn out to have been right."

I was looking out at the sea as he said that, as I am now. For a moment — for one moment only — I saw how the sea is always touching all the lands of the earth, and how it separates England from other lands, and is also the way we go to get to them. And I saw how heaven bends down and touches the earth and sea, so gently we can scarcely feel sure it is there. But the same sky rises over all, filled with stars by which we may chart our course.

I am a modern princess. Should I believe what a Gypsy may have said so many years ago?

I simply cannot say.

I think, now, I shall go and practice painting those palm trees. Dear Mr. Westall will see that I am trying to improve myself.

EPILOGUE

Scarcely a month after her eighteenth birthday, on Tuesday, June 20, 1837, Princess Victoria wrote in her real diary:

> I was awoke by Mamma who told me that the
> Archbishop of Canterbury and Lord Conyngham were
> here and wished to see me. I got out of bed and went
> into my sitting room (only in my dressing gown) and
> alone, and saw them. Lord Conyngham (the Lord
> Chamberlain) then acquainted me that my poor Uncle,
> the King, was no more, and had expired at 12 minutes
> past 2 this morning and consequently that I am Queen.

Because William IV had outlived her childhood, Victoria never required a Regent to rule for her. The ambitions of Sir John Conroy were dashed, and the young Queen steadfastly held herself apart from his influence from that day forward.

Victoria showed herself to be a poised, confident, energetic ruler. Educated in matters of State by Lord Melbourne, her first Prime Minister, and counseled by King Leopold and his old friend, Baron Stockmar, she became the first modern monarch of the United Kingdom. Political reform was promising to raise the fortunes of the common working people, and Victoria's personal virtues and idealism helped restore confidence in the Royal tradition. As a single, attractive Queen, she led a life filled, not only with government and world affairs, but also with dazzling social events, art, and music.

Then, when her cousin, Prince Albert of Saxe-Coburg-Gotha, came to visit, Victoria fell in love. Albert had also been a protégé of Leopold and Stockmar. He was well educated, philosophical, interested in science, as passionate about music and art as Victoria herself — and very handsome. They married on February 10, 1840.

As the "Victorian Era" began to blossom, Her Majesty's lively young family set the fashion for home life rather than courtly elegance. Victoria and Albert had nine children: Victoria ("Vicky"), the Princess Royal; the Prince of Wales, Albert Edward ("Bertie" — later, King Edward VII); Alice; Alfred ("Affie"); Helena ("Lenchen");

Louise; Arthur; Leopold; and Beatrice ("Baby"). The family spent a good deal of time away from London, at Osborne House on the Isle of Wight, and at Balmoral Castle in the Scottish Highlands. A visitor wrote of their lives away from Buckingham Palace:

> They live not merely like private gentlefolks, but like very small gentlefolks, small house, small rooms, small establishment. There are no soldiers, and the whole guard of the Sovereign and the whole Royal Family is a single policeman. . . . The Queen is running in and out of the house all day long, and often goes about alone, walks into the cottages, and sits down and chats with the old women. . . .

The Baroness Lehzen had retired from her role as Victoria's chief confidante once Prince Albert proved himself a strong husband and helpmate. Victoria came to rely on his insight and executive abilities to help her through the hundreds of messages and decisions required of her each day.

Victoria's early ties to the Whig (Liberal) party gave way, bit by bit, to a sense that the Crown should be a strong, continuous influence for good and stable values, "above" partisan politics, no matter which party was in power. Although always a staunch supporter of the (Protestant) Church of England, Victoria attempted to be fair and realistic about the contributions and rights of other religious groups. In 1837, before she'd ruled for even a year, she dubbed Sir Moses Montefiore the first Jewish Knight of the United Kingdom.

The Corn Laws, against imported grain, caused great harm in Catholic Ireland during the potato famine. When Prime Minister Robert Peel sacrificed his career to obtain their repeal, Victoria backed him. Though preoccupied with her frequent pregnancies and many little children, she had her own opinions. She supposed Ireland ought to be treated more like Scotland, where she and Albert felt quite at home, and she would not abide anti-Catholic preaching.

With all their hard work, Victoria and Albert still made time for art and music. Their frequent gifts to each other of paintings and sculpture "made" many artists' careers. Victoria took drawing lessons from nonsense poet and artist Edward Lear. The composer Felix Mendelssohn, too, was a guest at the palace. He said afterward that Prince Albert played the organ so ". . . that it would have done credit to any professional," and that Her Majesty sang ". . . really quite faultlessly, and with charming feeling and expression . . . as one seldom hears it done."

But sadness was too soon to lay claim to Victoria's

contentment. In the early winter of 1861, Prince Albert, generally healthy but overworked, contracted typhoid fever. (It is now thought he may also have suffered from stomach cancer.) His death, when they were both only forty-two years old, left Victoria changed forever by shock and sorrow. She never entirely recovered from the loss of the friend, husband, partner, and "dearest Master" she would always consider the most perfect of men.

Our most enduring image of Victoria is of Her Majesty in the black mourning clothes she wore for the remaining forty years of her life. For three entire years, in fact, she made almost no public appearances. The genuine grief of her subjects, meanwhile, gave way to impatience and disapproval; the people wanted their Queen to show herself strong despite her loss. Victoria could not do it, until the combined persuasion of her Prime Minister, Benjamin Disraeli, and Albert's and her old friend, their Scottish manservant, John Brown, convinced her that returning to a full and useful life was the best way to honor the dead.

From that time on, Victoria earned her reputation as "the Grandmother of Europe" by counseling and arranging marriages for her own children, nieces, and nephews among the Royal Families all across the Continent. She became more engaged than ever in extending British power and influence in international affairs. In 1875, Disraeli managed to have Parliament add to her other official titles, "Empress of India." With characteristic energy, Victoria took up the study of the Hindustani language, with tutoring from Abdul Karim, her private secretary, or *munshi*.

From the time she was thirteen, she kept a personal journal, writing sometimes ten pages in a day. She also managed to read and write an enormous number of letters. In 1868 and 1884, selections from her journal were published in book form. Unfortunately, she left instructions that when she died, her daughter, Princess Beatrice, was to go through her private papers and destroy anything inappropriate for publication. The princess, a Victorian of the most discreet and "proper" sort, destroyed a treasure of intelligent, sensitive historical commentary the likes of which we can only imagine.

By the end of her long life, Victoria was beloved and revered, not only in her own realm, but around the world. Her fiftieth anniversary as Queen was celebrated with a Golden Jubilee in 1887, followed by a Diamond Jubilee in 1897 — the only time she ever put off her widow's black and wore a white gown.

Victoria died on January 22, 1901. The poet Robert Bridges wrote, "It seemed as though the keystone had fallen out of the arch of heaven." In Parliament, Lord Salisbury said:

> She has been the greatest instance of government by example and by love, and it will never be forgotten how much she has done for the elevation of her people, not by . . . giving any command, but by the simple sight and contemplation of the brilliant qualities she exhibited in her exalted position. . . . She bridged over the great interval separating old England and new England. Other nations have had to pass through the same ordeal, but they seldom passed it so peacefully, easily, and with so much prosperity.

And British statesman, A.J. Balfour, observed, "She passed away, I believe, without a single enemy in the world, for even those who love not England love her."

HISTORICAL NOTE

Queen Victoria's sixty-three-year reign was the longest in England's history.

When Victoria was a child, the American and French revolutions and the Napoleonic wars were recent history. Gaslights, steam engines, and railways were new inventions. Photography was not introduced until 1839, and the first telegraph line in England, not until 1844.

Working-class men and women could not participate in elections; neither could Roman Catholics, Jews, or members of other religious minorities. The fast-growing new industrial cities could not send their own representatives to Parliament. There were no laws to protect children from being forced into mining or factory labor, or to guarantee them adequate food, shelter, or schooling. Slavery was still legal in the United Kingdom until 1833.

By the time of Victoria's death in 1901, the first telephones, electric lights, typewriters, automobiles, and radios had been introduced — not to mention matches and coat hangers! Religious and racial bigotry was not extinguished, but it was not so firmly supported by the law. It would be only a couple of years until the Wright brothers' first airplane took to the sky, and twenty-seven years until all British women won the vote.

Many of the "classic" authors, composers, and artists were created by the Victorian era, and many worked and taught as Her Majesty's subjects and admirers. Queen Victoria herself was an avid "fan" of the music of Rossini, Bellini, Liszt, Mendelssohn, and Wagner. She adored the ballerina Maria Taglioni, and, while visiting the French Empress Eugenie on the Riviera, was pleased to meet the famous actress Sarah Bernhardt. By the end of the century, the theater was enlivened by Gilbert and Sullivan, George Bernard Shaw, and Oscar Wilde.

Some Victorian painters are still sometimes noted for the sentimentality of their work, but the country landscapes of John Constable are clear and natural, while J.M.W. Turner used light and color in ways that opened the eyes of the Impressionists to come. And although nostalgia for the preindustrial past popularized the Gothic and pre-Raphaelite styles, progress could not be turned back. Crowded cities and disappearing countrysides demanded buildings that could expand upward. Architecture changed forever with the Victorians' development of iron — and later, steel — beams, and the ability to make larger, stronger sheets of window glass. Prince Albert's Great Exhibition, an amazing showcase for all these arts and technological advances, was held in the Crystal Palace, a giant "greenhouse" that enclosed full-grown trees.

Before Victoria's time, very few books had been written for — or about — child readers, but that was to change. Charlotte Brontë's *Jane Eyre* came out in 1847, Lewis Carroll's *Alice's Adventures in Wonderland* and *Through the Looking-Glass* were published in 1865 and 1871, respectively. His friend George Macdonald's *The Princess and the Goblin* (1872) is a fairy story about a royal child not unlike Victoria — surrounded by dangers but protected by the love of loyal common folk. Robert Louis Stevenson's *Treasure Island* (1883) is as thrilling now as ever, his *A Child's Garden of Verses* (1885) still one of the most popular poetry collections. Charles Dickens's wry and compassionate *Oliver Twist* (1838) and *A Christmas Carol* (1843), and Charles Kingsley's *The Water-Babies* (1863) appealed for better living conditions for the poor. *The Blue Fairy Book* by Andrew Lang (1889) began a long series of "color fairy" retellings of tales from many lands. And the success of the late-Victorian Rudyard Kipling's *Jungle Books* (1894 and 1895) and *Just So Stories* (1902) celebrated British imperialism in India and Africa.

Children of all classes led lives far different from what is usual nowadays. Even those who did not have to go to work spent their early years in the "nursery" and home schoolroom under the care of a governess, and saw little of their own parents. Not all homes had running water. Though flush toilets had been invented in 1777, they were not common for another hundred years. Coal fires provided rather unreliable heat — and a great deal of polluted air.

Medical knowledge was greatly improving public health, though. When Victoria was a child, conservative physicians were still reluctant to accept the idea that the blood circulated through the body, and they thought fevers were caused by patient's having too much blood. Then, Louis Pasteur discovered that many diseases were actually bacterial infections, an observation that revolutionized hygiene and surgery. The Duke of Kent saw to it that his precious child was inoculated against smallpox. Joseph Lister proved that sterilizing instruments and operating rooms with heat or carbolic acid dramatically reduced the postsurgical death rate. Queen Victoria herself helped popularize the use of chloroform as an anesthetic — her doctors gave it to her during the births of her younger children. Even the use of plaster casts on broken bones was a Victorian innovation.

During the same years when civilization was making all these advances, unfortunately, self-righteousness and greed too often combined with "improved" weaponry in the dark side of British success: The glories of the Empire included British invasions around the world. The sun never set on Her Majesty's Army and Navy. In India, Egypt, Sudan, the Crimea, Burma, China, South Africa, and Central America, native societies resisted in vain. Victorian citizens believed earnestly that they owed it to the world to make war to "improve" conditions for "savage" nations. In the process, they took for themselves the riches of the continents. No wonder that little England was the wealthiest country in the history of the world! In turn, the blood-tainted profits from Asia and Africa helped develop Canada, British Guiana (now Belize), the West Indies, Australia, New Zealand, Singapore, and Hong Kong.

Yet it is undeniable: In England and all its dominions, Victorian common sense, efficiency, and conscientious intentions did allow a new stability for agriculture and industry. The Empire was often arrogant, brutal, racist, and blind to the values and rights of other cultures. Still, the order Great Britain embodied during the nineteenth century allowed the world to learn how to feed, clothe, heal, and educate more of its children than ever before. The highest ideals of Victoria's people are still admired. By means of their energy and courage, the idea and realization of liberty took root in lands and social classes that had never dared pursue such a dream.

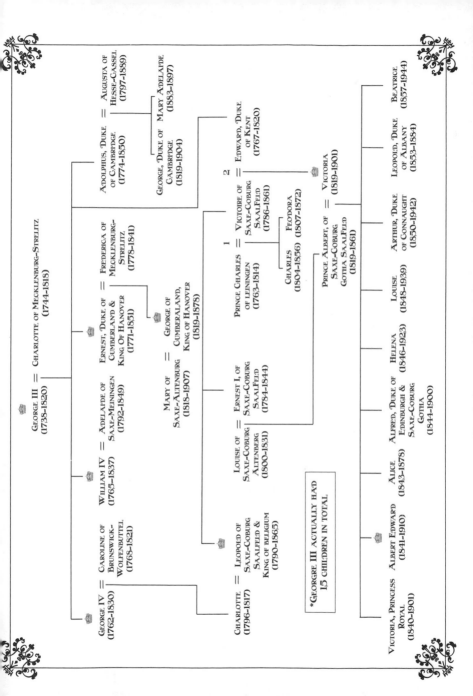

The Hanover-Coburg Family Tree

The Hanover dynasty began with King George I, Victoria's great-great paternal grandfather, who was a German descendant of King James I of England. Victoria's mother belonged to the Saxe-Coburg family of royals who ruled a territory in the German region known as Thuringia. British custom and law provided that members of the royal family could not choose to marry Catholics or commoners, and could not marry at all without the monarch's consent. Therefore, the most eligible matches were often found among the same few noble houses of Europe. Hence, intermarriage among even first cousins, as with Victoria and Albert, was not uncommon. The chart illustrates the growth and interconnections of these two family lines. The crown symbol indicates those who ruled. Double lines represent marriages; single lines indicate parentage. Dates of births and deaths (when available) are noted.

King George III

Victoria's paternal grandfather; born 1738, crowned 1760, died 1820.

Queen Charlotte ("Grandma'am")

Princess of Mecklenburg-Strelitz; born 1744, married George III. They had fifteen children–six girls and nine boys of whom two (Octavius and Alfred) died as toddlers. She died in 1818.

Edward Augustus, Duke of Kent

Fourth son and fifth child of George III and Queen Charlotte; born 1767. In 1799, Prince Edward was made Duke of Kent and Strathearn and Earl of Dublin. In 1818, he married the Dowager Princess Victoire of Leiningen, making her Duchess of Kent. Their child, Princess Victoria, was born in 1819. The Duke died after a brief illness in 1820, when Victoria was only eight months old.

VICTOIRE OF SAXE-COBURG AND SAALFELD, DUCHESS OF KENT

Victoria's mother, sister of Prince Leopold. Born 1786; married at seventeen to Prince Emich Charles of Leiningen, who was twenty-three years older than she, and when he died, he left her a widow with two children (Charles and Feodora). When she was thirty-two, she married the Duke of Kent and moved to England. She was not popular with her royal in-laws. She died in 1861.

PRINCE CHARLES OF LEININGEN

Victoria's half-brother; born 1804, died 1856.

PRINCESS FEODORA OF LEININGEN "FEO"

Victoria's half-sister; married Prince Ernest of Hohenlohe-Langenburg; born 1807, died 1872.

ALEXANDRINA VICTORIA

Only child of Edward Augustus, Duke of Kent, and Victoire of Saxe-Coburg. Born May 24, 1819, she inherited the throne of England at age eighteen from her uncle, King William IV. In February 1840, she married her cousin Albert, Prince of Saxe-Coburg and Gotha. Her reign lasted for sixty-three years until her death in 1901.

ALBERT, PRINCE OF SAXE-COBURG AND GOTHA

Younger son of Duke Ernest, nephew of Duchess of Kent and King Leopold; born 1819, he married his cousin, Victoria, in 1840, and together they had nine children before his death in 1861.

An English wood engraving of a demure, fifteen-year-old Princess Victoria made from a drawing done by J. R. Herbert at Kensington Palace in March 1834.

Portrayed here in oil on canvas painting by Mary Gow, are the Archbishop of Canterbury (left) and the Lord Chamberlain (kneeling) on the morning of June 20, 1837, as they came to inform the young Princess Victoria of her accession to the throne.

Shown above are Victoria (center) in 1837 surrounded by some of her family members. Also pictured are Victoria's mother, the Duchess of Kent (top), her grandmother (bottom), her half-sister, Feodora (left), and her half-brother, Charles.

Kensington Palace in London, England, as photographed by Michael Boys in November of 1991. Queen Victoria was born here on May 14, 1819, and lived here throughout her childhood. The State Apartments have since been restored to their former eighteenth-century grandeur. Today, several of the staterooms are still open to the public.

This photograph, taken on June 2, 1949, is of Victoria's bedroom in the State Apartments at Kensington Palace. It was here that Victoria was awakened in the early hours of June 20, 1837, with the news of her accession to the throne. She then made an unprecedented move to Buckingham Palace and ruled her kingdom from there.

This picture of Victoria and her husband, by Robert Fenton, circa 1854, was the first photograph ever taken of her. Prince Albert and Victoria were wed in 1840, and they remained happily married until Albert's death in 1861.

Balmoral Castle in Aberdeen, Scotland. Balmoral was purchased in 1846 by Prince Albert, and it was home to him and Victoria during much of their marriage. Queen Victoria often visited the Scottish Highlands with her family, especially after Albert's death, and the building is still a popular retreat for the present-day royal family.

A modern map of Great Britain.

This undated photograph shows the ornate Imperial State Crown, which was created specifically for Queen Victoria of England.

The first postage stamp, known as the Penny Black, pictures Queen Victoria and was created in May 1840. It was black in color and had a denomination of one cent, hence its name. Since that time all regular stamp issues have portrayed the reigning king or queen.

Seen here in her royal garb, this photographic portrait of Victoria was taken in the fiftieth year of her reign as the Queen of the United Kingdom of Great Britain and Ireland, 1887. Her sixty-three-year reign remains the longest in British history.

This photograph displays Osborne House, on the Isle of Wight, circa 1900. In 1845, Queen Victoria and Prince Albert bought Osborne House and its 1,000 acres as a retreat. Victoria died there in 1901. Since her death, little has changed at Osborne House and many of the royal couple's possessions, photographs, and paintings are still there.

Glossary of Characters

Victoria's Family

Queen Adelaide — Victoria's aunt; wife of William IV.

Lord Adolphus Fitzclarence — Son of William IV.

Adolphus, Duke of Cambridge — Victoria's uncle; son of George III.

Prince Albert of Saxe-Coburg and Gotha — son of Ernest I;
Victoria's cousin, whom she married in 1840.

Princess Amelia — youngest daughter of George III.

Augusta of Cambridge — Victoria's cousin.

Princess Augusta — Victoria's aunt; daughter of George III.

Captain Augustus and Miss d'Este — children of the Duke of Sussex.

Augustus Frederick, Duke of Sussex — son of George III.

Prince Charles of Leiningen — Victoria's half-brother.

Princess Charlotte — only child of King George IV; married to Prince
Leopold of Saxe-Coburg and Saalfeld.

Queen Charlotte ("Grandma'am") — Victoria's paternal grandmother;
wife of George III.

Edward Augustus, Duke of Kent — Victoria's father; son of George III.

Princess Elizabeth — Victoria's aunt; daughter of George III.

Ernest, Duke of Cumberland — Victoria's uncle; son of George III.

Ernest, Prince of Hohenlohe-Langenburg — husband of Victoria's
half-sister, Princess Feodora of Leiningen.

Ernest I, of Saxe-Coburg Saalfeld — (1) Duchess of Kent's and Prince
Leopold's older brother; (2) his son, Albert's elder brother.

Princess Feodora of Leiningen — Victoria's half-sister.

Frederick, Duke of York — Victoria's uncle; son of George III.

King George III — Victoria's grandfather.

King George IV — Victoria's uncle; son of George III.

Prince George of Cumberland — Victoria's cousin; son of Duke Ernest.

Prince Leopold of Saxe-Coburg and Saalfeld — Victoria's uncle and mentor; brother of Duchess of Kent.

Princess Sophia — Victoria's aunt; daughter of George III.

Victoire of Saxe-Coburg and Saalfeld, Duchess of Kent — Victoria's mother; sister of Prince Leopold.

King William IV (Duke of Clarence) — Victoria's uncle; son of George III.

FRIENDS, ATTENDANTS, AND ASSOCIATES

Mrs. Arbuthnot — friend of the Duchess of Kent.

Madame Bou[r]din — Victoria's dancing teacher.

Mrs. Brock ("Brocky") — Victoria's nurse.

Lord Brougham — Whig Member of Parliament.

Sir John Conroy — the Duchess of Kent's financial comptroller.

Victoire Conroy — daughter of Sir John Conroy.

Lady Conyngham — wife of the Lord Chamberlain.

Mr. (Thomas) Coutts — banker for Victoria's mother.

Reverend George Davys — Victoria's tutor.

Queen Maria da Gloria of Portugal — married Prince Ferdinand of Coburg, Victoria's cousin.

Princess Dorothea de Lieven — wife of the Russian ambassador to George IV's court.

Baroness de Spaeth — lady in waiting to Victoria's mother.

Lord John Elphinstone — officer in the Royal Horse Guards.

Bishop Fisher of Salisbury — uncle of Sir John Conroy's wife.

Lady Catherine Jenkinson — lady in waiting to Victoria's mother.

Mrs. Louis — Leopold's Claremont housekeeper.

Baroness Louise Lehzen — Victoria's governess.

Sir Moses Montefiore — Prince Leopold's friend.

Duchess of Northumberland — Victoria's governess.

Robert Owen — pioneer of the cooperative movement.

Mr. John Sale — Victoria's music instructor.

Dr. Christian von Stockmar — Leopold's physician.

Arthur Wellesley, Duke of Wellington — Tory Prime Minister and commander-in-chief.

Mr. Richard Westall — Victoria's art instructor.

Family Pets

Dash — Victoria's mother's tan-and-white King Charles spaniel.

Fanny — Victoria's black-and-tan terrier.

Rosa — Victoria's grey pony.

About the Author

When she was growing up, some of Anna Kirwan's favorite books were by Victorian authors Lewis Carroll and George MacDonald. Kirwan spent a lot of time reading.

"I loved books and generally managed to keep one I was enjoying with me all the time," she says. "I even read whenever I had a few moments of 'waiting' time — on bus rides, for example, and during the commercial breaks and boring parts of TV shows."

Ms. Kirwan has written four previous books for young readers — *The Jewel of Life*, a fantasy novel, and the Girlhood Journeys' *Juliet* series, about a medieval family. She has written short stories and poems for adults as well as children.

"When I started my research for *Victoria, May Blossom of Britannia*, I didn't know how much I would like the Princess Victoria," the author recalls. "But, after all, her life was the inspiration for many authors whose books touched my heart and amused me when I was a kid."

She explains, "I would like my readers to understand that this book is fiction based on history. There are several places in the story where I have used my novelist's imagination and altered details or filled in missing pieces of historical puzzles. For example," she says, "I purposely combined into one the two interviews Victoria actually had with the bishops.

"It is a fact that in October 1830, Victoria did observe some inappropriate 'familiarity' in Sir John Conroy's treatment of her mother, and the upset over it did result in the dismissal of the Baroness de Spaeth. However, what actually happened is not known, so I have given the story my interpretation. I also exercised creative license on the character of Prince George of Cumberland, to make him seem 'horrid' to Victoria, who was not used to playing with boys."

Anna Kirwan is the mother of a daughter and two sons. She lives in Northampton, Massachusetts, where she leads writing workshops and works as a freelance editor. She is an executive board member of Amherst Writers and Artists and the AWA Press.

ACKNOWLEDGMENTS

I am grateful for the encouragement and assistance of many friends and poets. Michael Wolff has been especially useful, as usual. Jane Yolen and David Stemple mended a wing for me. Ellie Cook, *sine qua non*. Wise and patient Ginger Knowlton, patient and wise Sonia Black, panic-averting Danielle Denega; AWA ears eyes hearts; *mes delices*, Korena, Max, Rob; Elizabeth, Karen, Mary-Beth, Susan, Bill — Thank you.

Cover painting by Tim O'Brien

Page 206: Victoria at age fifteen, North Wind Picture Archives, Alfred, Maine.

Page 207: Victoria's accession, Archive Photos, New York, New York.

Page 208: Victoria and family members, Culver Pictures, Inc., New York, New York.

Page 209: Kensington Palace, Corbis Images, New York, New York.

Page 209: Victoria's bedchamber, Archive Photos, New York, New York.

Page 210: Victoria and Albert, Archive Photos, New York, New York.

Page 211: Balmoral Castle, Culver Pictures, New York, New York.

Page 211: Map of Great Britain by James McMahon.

Page 212: Crown, Bettman Archive/Corbis Images, New York, New York.

Page 212: Postage stamp, The Granger Collection, New York, New York.

Page 213: Portrait of Victoria, 1887, Archive Photos, New York, New York.

Page 213: Osborne House, Archive Photos, New York, New York.

Other books in The Royal Diaries series

Elizabeth I
Red Rose of the House of Tudor
by Kathryn Lasky

Cleopatra VII
Daughter of the Nile
Kristiana Gregory

Isabel
Jewel of Castilla
by Carolyn Meyer

Marie Antoinette
Princess of Versailles
by Kathryn Lasky

Anastasia
The Last Grand Duchess
by Carolyn Meyer

Nzingha
Warrior Queen of Matamba
by Patricia C. McKissack

KAIULANI
The People's Princess
by Ellen Emerson White

LADY OF CH'IAO KUO
Warrior of the South
by Laurence Yep

For my aunts and uncles.

While The Royal Diaries are based on real royal figures
and actual historical events, some situations and people
in the book are fictional, created by the author.

ISBN 0-439-21598-6

12 11 10 9 8 7 6 5 4 3 2 1   01 02 03 04 05

The text type in this book was set in Augereau.
The display type was set in Rogers.
Book design by Elizabeth B. Parisi.

Printed in the U.S.A.
First printing, November 2001